All Good Bye's Ain't Gone

An Urban Love Story

C. Yusef Wells

Edited by Myla Twillie

This book is dedicated to my brother Nelson Wells. And a special tribute and eternal salute to all the Brothers and Sisters from every neighborhood, or ghetto in the entire world who have departed this life. May their transition be peaceful with spaciousness and light in the grave. May the Creator of all that exists bestow His mercy upon them. May he forgive them their wrong and reward them for their good. Especially those souls from the Village of Slauson. And to those from within a section of the Village that I recall and those that I may have forgotten.

Nut, Donnie D., Charlie Fats, Tommy Bracey, George Wiley, Lee J.R. Johnson, Big Rich Williams, David Wiley, Harold Soap Ricks, Claudia Hunter Ricks, Junie Williams, Gregory Fat Mack, Sunny Williams, Murray M.C. Skillet, Ronnie Barrett, Eddie Moon Dog Davis, Leon Rayford, Brenda Rayford, Ronnie V., Shelly Dennis, Ronnie Mack, Clarence Baby Brother, Calvin Twenty-Cent Lewis, Bernard Wilhite, Papoose, Marshall Jones, Carnell Brown, Charles Dickson, Danny Boy Horn, K.K. Horn, Floyd Horn, Andrew Conway, Benny B.C. Childs, Nathan-Larry-Lonnie Evans, Paul Norwood, Gloria Perkins, George Lil Abner Norris, Charlie Fats Norris, Tommy Hog Jaws Choctaw, Renay Choctaw, Hawk, Doc, Gorman Fish Thomas, Sandra Nelson, Pig, Porter Saturday Morning, Jackie Lee, Murry F., Willie the Wolf, Shorty, T.L. Yoakum, Gary D., Beverly Bray, Dorothy Johnson, Raymond Johnson, Brah Boy, Donna Faye, Kitty Broadnax, Rhonda Sanders, Sandra Jefferson, Mary Peachtree, Yvonne Hardy, Elizabeth Tippins, George Davis, Jeanie Davis, Lo-Lo Davis, Donald Adams, Lottie Adams, Langry Winston, Lorraine McGee, Teddy McGee, Big Stan, Freda Davis, Gaynell, Elijah Jenkins, Geraldine Jenkins and Bobby Houston.

Contents

A very special tribute to Myla Twillie and Outsource Ink, Y. Choctaw, Lonnie J, Muhamed Abdula, Fantastic Designs, TeErra Johnson, Stephanie "Tootsie" Nieves, Kumasi, Khalid Shaw, Poppa Shaw, LaKeysha Pack, D'xishari Khalfani and to all of my readers who have supported and encouraged me to continue my writing. Your constructive energy will never be obliterated. You are appreciated.

"When We Thought We Knew Everything"

A Scholar asked a wise man...
After many years of study I wish to know when
shall I attain full knowledge of everything?

The wise man replied..
You will obtain complete knowledge of
everything when you get to the point where you
realize that you know NOTHING.

Author's Glossary

The following terms have appeared throughout the story in bold italicized print. The terms are from a vernacular popular in the late sixties and seventies, some of which are used today, especially amongst people of the nightlife.

Abe in Bosom – Lucky

Acapulco Gold – Potent strain of marijuana.

Booster – Male or female who steals merchandise.

Broke Luck – Made first dollar.

Cop and Blow – To gain and then loose.

Cop jive – Understand game.

Dandy – A man devoted to style and neat fashion.

Ends – Money.

Five-O – Police.

Full Nelson – Wrestling headlock.

Gorilla Mack – Pimp that uses muscle and force on his women.

Hari Kari – Suicide.

High signed – Boasted or bragged.

Ho Boots – Knee high leather boots.

Hog – A large car.

Kennedy Swoop – Popular processed styled hair.

Kite – A note or a letter.

Kotch Ball Card Tournament – A high stakes tournament where the card game Kotch is played.

Lace Up – To teach.

Long in tooth – Old

Mack Daddy – Smooth talking pimp.

Mark – A targeted victim of a crime.

Mich – Roll of counterfeit or play money with a real large bill on top.

Monkey On Back – Drug habit.

Pigeon Drop, Donation, and 3 Card Monte – Various con games.

Polly Pop – Soda or Kool-Aid

Rollers/Five-o – Police.

Rosco – A gun.

Sawbuck – A ten dollar bill.

Sex Charge – Excuse for a pimp to have free sex.

Smooth Mack – Pimp that uses verbal persuasion.

Snow Bunny – White woman.

Sting – A move where money is made.

T's – Crooked dice.

The Drag – Con game.

The Front – Area in Watts where heroine was sold.

The Hawk – the wind; cold weather.

The Stroll – Street or avenue where prostitutes solicit their service.

Trick Willie – One who pays for sex.

Vic – A victim of a scam.

Vogues – Tires generally worn on a Cadillac.

White Slavery – The mann act. Transporting women across state lines for immoral reasons.

Wood – Fleetwood Cadillac

Chapter 1

MaDear

The crimson days of sweat and Polly Pop played last tag and kissed the falling leaves of orange and yellow as the summer of '64 faded way too soon, as summer breaks always did. The carefree days of slumber were over and the pursuit of education and eventual graduation were at hand.

Seventeen-year old Dandy Dixon, or Dandy-Dee as he was more commonly known, stood slightly to the left of the cracked mirror on the dresser in the bedroom he shared with his two nephews, Jamal and Joshua. He was checking his self out as he dressed for the first day of school.

The two bedroom wood-framed house was handed down to him and his older brother Tyrone, his wife Freda and their two sons with the passing of both their parents. Their 'Pops' was a career military man that was killed in action during the early fifties in the Korean War. Their mother, 'MaDear', had passed just two years earlier in 1962 at a young age due to complications from pneumonia. Mrs. Margaret Dixon never re-married and raised her two sons with a gentle loving heart and cast iron hands. She was a medium sized woman, with reddish-brown complexion and a presence as huge as all outdoors that commanded attention from her sons and anyone else she encountered.

Staring in the mirror Dandy's mind flashed back a few years and smiled as he recalled a cold winter morning bundled up in bed covers as his mother entered the room. "Boy! What are you doing in that bed? Get your behind up and get dressed for school."

"It's too cold MaDear, I'm not going." He declared.

"Okay" she replied calmly as she left the room. He closed his eyes and in a flash MaDear was pouring ice-cold water all over his head. He leaped out of bed like a bullfrog and stood erect on the hardwood floor shivering. "Oh, so your butt is up now I see!" she bellowed with a pointed finger in his face she admonished. "Let me tell you what you are going to do in life, what you had better do."

"Yes MaDear" he uttered respectfully.

"First off, you're going to school this morning and every day hereafter."

Dandy nodded in agreement.

"Don't be nodding your head, speak up like a young man. I remind you of things because I love you and it's my responsibility to tell you what's best for you. Next I want you to always remember to be respectful to your elders. Always bless your food. And get on those knees every day and say a thankful morning prayer, and a good night prayer. Clean yourself when you're dirty and put clean underwear on, you never know when you may have to go to the hospital or see a doctor. You won't be embarrassing me or yourself, having the nurses all over town saying Mrs. Dixon's boy wears filthy, nasty drawers. I know I raised you to do these things; I'm just reminding you. And finally, you will walk across somebody's stage and get your diploma. Am I understood!"?

"Yes MaDear," he promised…"Yes MaDear" he repeated to himself as he snapped out of the daydream with a broad smile.

Two extremely worn pairs of jeans, blue Levi's and black Frisco's stood straight up on the back wall by their self, stiff, and shiny with summer's grime; it was a sin for him and his friends to allow their jeans to be washed. They had served him well all summer, but now his focus was on dressier attire.

He opened the closet and reached for a pair of silk and wool slacks and an Italian turtle neck sweater, he was looking for his brown biscuit toe Stacy's when Freda entered the room and advised. "You better hurry up Dandy, it's nearly 7:30."

"Thanks sis, I'm on it."

Looking at the jeans she sighed. "I can finally wash those jeans! MaDear would have never allowed you to wear those dirty things this long. "

"You're right Sis. And I would give an arm, both legs, and an eye if washing them would bring her back." He stated matter-of-factly.

Freda smiled and left holding the jeans with thumb and fingers.

Now he scurried to get dressed. He was always a neat dresser in school. His MaDear always told him to live up to the name her brother chose for him because it meant a man who was devoted to style and neatness. She wasn't able to purchase hi-fashion clothes regularly, but she did the best she could living off of her husband's pension and doing days work. When she passed Tyrone looked out for his baby brother but he had a wife and two young sons to care for, his job at the post office paid well but Dandy chose to hustle for extra clothes he desired.

He had a wardrobe of slacks, shirts, Hoodlum Priest suits and Cut-Away coats and several leather jackets. His entrepreneurial venture, dealing weed, provided extra money for his clothes and hopefully a low rider he was saving up for. He expected to be rolling by the next semester.

3

He was doing well in his world and thought he knew all about life. But it was about to evolve into the vast new world of reality. It was about to bust wide open, and open up it did!

Chapter 2

Eye Candy

The hardwood floors of the science building shined like new money and smelled of fresh wax. Blurred shadows cast reflections of students flowing with chatter, laughter, and gossip bouncing off the walls. This was one of four buildings that comprised what students called "The Mont", formally titled, Fremont High.

After obtaining a list of required subjects from the Administration building, each individual hurried about the task of registering into their mandatory classes at their desired times of choice. Everyone had seven periods to fill, actually five academic classes because lunch and gym were for everyone. Most students moved along at a rapid pace and some shuffled along doing a slow drag trying to be cool.

One such person was Dandy Dee. School wasn't something he wanted to do; it was something he had to do for his mother's sake. His dress was sharp like some students, some were casually clean, and a few didn't wear brand new outfits but their clothes were impeccably washed and ironed. Most teens relied on three occasions to adorn and show off new clothes – Christmas, Easter Sunday, and the new semester of school. And some were less fortunate.

The white enrollment card flapped in one hand with every sliding glide as Dandy surveyed the hall looking for a science class that wasn't filled. He had locked down English, Math, History, and Geography classes. Science, the one he dreaded most, was last.

Abruptly his carefree pace hit slow motion as he peeped two young ladies approaching him. His antennas went up, his brown eyes focused and his heart accelerated. He put his registration card in his hip pocket and cupped his hands to pat his natural in shape. Hoping to meet them with a sparkling smile and a slick line of introduction.

They stepped in stride like two Maltese kittens. One had skin the color of honey in sunlight, a tiny black mole at the corner of her moist lips and a short curly natural that she wore well. She was draped in a conservative pastel blouse and loosely fitted A-shaped skirt. Her friend had a dark complexion as smooth as silk, a freshly frosted perm, and almond shaped eyes that were reading the classroom numbers. A statuesque figure that filled a burgundy tight skirt like a hand in a glove, perfectly paired with a soft pink cashmere sweater.

Dandy's head was spinning like a top as he assessed these two females that carried an air of maturity that the other fifteen to seventeen years olds didn't have. Their heels click-clacked right on into room S-189 before he could make his presence known. He made a quick inspection of the semester program from his back pocket.

"Bingo!" he yelled as his forearms hit his waistline and shrugged his shoulders up…"Science – Room S189 Mrs. Boyle – 5th period. "

Entering the classroom with coolness and a serious face he cleared his throat as he approached the teacher's desk and spoke. "Good morning, I would like to enroll in this class."

Mrs. Boyle was fiftyish and extremely hard on the eyes but neither she nor science was his target, one of the two girls was. The instructor had been lurking over a pair of inch thick bifocals. After a pause she spoke, "Sorry young man, this class is filled but I have another science class at 6th period."

Disappointed, he slurred, "thank you anyway" and turned towards the exit scanning the room hoping to catch a last glimpse of the "Queens" but a few steps found him at the exit. He never noticed them again in the next few weeks of school. Not the pretty one with the plain demeanor, or her cute friend with the bombshell body. He felt like a desert traveller who spotted an oasis that turned out to be a mirage.

School was progressing and rewarding in more ways than one. The young ladies he had known before treated him royally and the money he was stacking with his off-campus weed sales was another. The bell for nutrition rang and ended the dull history lecture and his daydreams. MaDear's words redundantly spoke, "Oh, you're walking across somebody's stage and get a diploma." As young as he was, he understood the value of having a word and his promise to his mother would not be broken.

He swiftly gathered his notepad and books and shot down the hallway to place them in his locker. Deciding not to eat in the cafeteria he went to the snack line and bought a grill cheese toast and a sweet roll along with a carton of milk. He then proceeded to the "Quad", a fountain in the middle of the campus, where the majority of students ate, studied, gossiped, and high-signed.

Dandy had just polished off his snack when he observed a slightly pudgy and always smiling friend of his named Stanley Dewberry. Stanley's grin broadened as he saw Dandy looking his way. Upon approach Stanley greeted him with outstretched palms up hands, Dandy slapped hands and Stanley began, "Hey Dandy Dee! What's happening baby boy?"

"You got the best hand home boy."

With serious face and roving eyes Stanley whispered, "I need three lids, can you come by my ole man's store after school?"

"Be there around five." Dandy assured.

Stanley flashed a smile, took a step then snapped his finger then added "By the way, you may not have noticed her but there's a certain young lady that's been worrying me to death about meeting you. She's standing across the quad over there." Pointing to the same two ladies Dandy saw the first day of school.

They were looking their way and covering their mouths up with an obvious attempt to hide the whispers.

"Say!" Dandy broke out with big eyes. "What is the chick's name in the plaid dress and loafers?"

"That's my girl, Crystal Jones, her friend is Priscilla Parker. She is the one who wants to meet you."

Briskly they strolled over to the girls. Upon close observation Priscilla was sexy and cute. Her smile was like white frosting on a cake. Definitely the eye catcher he saw on day one and the first to speak.

"Hello" she purred.

"What's happening young lady?" Dandy returned.

"Just wanted to be introduced to you, this is my friend Crystal."

Immediately Crystal replied, "And your name?"

"I'm Dandy Dee, I saw you two beautiful sisters the first day of school but hadn't had the pleasure of eye-to-eye conversation."

Crystal was ultra fine even in the conservative clothes she wore. Very alluring.

"We saw you too." Priscilla interjected.

Before another word was spoken Stanley broke in. "We were wondering if we could escort you ladies to the after school dance Friday, weren't we Dandy?"

"Ah, of course we were." Dandy confirmed slowly taking his eyes off Crystal.

Before anyone could speak the bell rang ending lunch. The girls grabbed their books while confirming. "That's a promise, we have a date. The four of us Friday."

Crystal was silent but her smile was in the affirmative.

See you tonight Dee," Stanley said and added "I gotta catch my art class."

Dandy assured, "Right, later on tonight." Little did Dandy know that it would be the last time he would see Stanley Dewberry.

***

After school Dandy hung his outfit up and changed into a casual pair of corduroy pants and a shirt. Before he finished getting dressed Tyrone asked his brother if he intended to go to college after graduation.

Dandy replied, "Yeah Ty, I been thinking about it but I'm not sure what I want to major in, not yet anyway."

"That's cool, let's see when the time comes. If you don't, I can see about getting you on at the post office. It's a government gig with benefits."

"Thanks big brah, I gotta make a run, be back later."

***

The night air was windy, not Chicago windy, but Santa Ana Winds windy. He placed a high brimmed Beaver Fedora precisely on tops of his fro, gave it a complementing ace-deuce twist and a final look of approval.

His nephews Jamal and Josh gazed at the uncle they loved so dearly.

"Bring me that long leather piece Jamal," as he pointed to a hook on the back of the closet door.

Both boys scuffled over the assignment. Dandy smiled at the courage of Joshua who was a half-foot shorter than his brother.

"All right! Hold up and be cool." He demanded, "I'll get it myself," as he swirled the coat on and dug into his pocket before hitting the back door and came up with two new silver dollars and said, "One apiece, you're brothers and you fight for each other, not with one another."

With wide eyes they chanted in perfect harmony, "Yes sir Uncle Dandy, and thanks."

The streetlights were dim with half functioning and the other half busted by rocks or had simply played out. The leather coat on his back served him well shielding the wind that pressed his back and pushed him to the end of the block in record time. Approaching San Pedro St. he rounded the corner of 66th St. and proceeded down the narrow but busy street towards Stanley's fathers record shop.

"Dandy!" A voice screeched out, "moving mighty fast son…too fast to holler at the ole man." Schoolboy declared as he stood in the doorway of his storefront where there was a shoeshine parlor. Inside, the walls were lined with autographed photos of Schoolboy and just about every notable musician, entertainer, boxer, and pimp from the forty's and fifty's. A jukebox lit the dim room but a pull of the curtain divider would have revealed a baby casino with a couch, dice table and three of four card tables.

"Sorry School, it was nothing personal I was dealing with the hawk and I'm making a delivery."

Schoolboy's teeth gripped the stem of the pipe he was gnawing on and spoke out of one side of his mouth. "What did I tell you about that word 'sorry'? Beg a pardon, ask forgiveness, or say you didn't mean to say this or that, but never say 'sorry'."

Dandy nodded in agreement as "School" continued.

"Fast as you was stepping it must be important business, you had better move on, we can cut it up later. Right?"

"Yes sir." Dandy agreed while swinging out the door and spinning back on down San Pedro St. towards Florence Avenue where the record-shop was a few storefronts away.

Dandy smiled on the inside as he thought about Schoolboy. Rumor had it that he couldn't read or write but he could count money better than a banker and there wasn't a question about life that he didn't have an answer to. He was the 'Old Master'. School and Dandy's father were the best of pals growing up. Dandy's father joined the army and School took to the streets with finesse.

A sharp breeze whipped past his ear and snapped him back to his surroundings. Really starting to get cold now, he said to his self. One day I'll drive up and down this track in my low-rider, he added as the 49 Maple, the bus that serviced San Pedro Street, blew past him leaving a warm comforting breeze from it's engine. He had five hundred and fifty dollars stashed for his ride and by the end of the semester he would have a grand. Enough for a clean one he surmised.

Reaching Sixty-Eighth Street he saw "Sweetmeat", and his fellow wine-o partners properly seated on milk crates that lined the front of Lee's Liquor Store. They sat erect with crossed legs as if they were guests on the White House porch.

Dandy waived from across the street while passing.

Sweetmeat yelled, "Boy" I swear you remind me of my brother Nulson," as he always did when he was tipsy.

And Dandy corrected him as he always did in fun, "Give Nelson my regards."

"His name is Nulson, N.E.L.S.O.N." Sweetmeat emphasized.

"Okay Sweetmeat, Nulson. See you later." Dandy hollered and kept on down Pedro.

At Sixty-Ninth Street in front of the Mexican Food Café he bumped into a group of guys he had grown up with.

"Dandy Dee! My lil homie, what's whipping besides the wind?" A brother named 'Knock Out Bell' yelled.

"You got it Bell. Nothing shaking but the leaves on the trees." Dandy shot back with a smile and added to the three others, "What's happening y'all?"

"Not much Dee," Crook, Bracey, and Shack Daddy cracked in unison.

Bell was a member of the Renegades and the others were members of the Le Monsieur's. Two of several chapters of a club that some considered a gang called The Slausons. Past years had eared Leonard Bell his moniker. At six foot three and two hundred thirty pounds plus his hands were lightening fast and knock out dangerous. But gentle as a lame if he liked you. Dandy had known him most of his life and they were very close because they grew up next door to each other. He was a few years older than Dandy and a year or two under Tyrone.

Dandy pulled out a stick of weed and gave it to Bell, "Here fire this up, I gotta go see Stanley at the record-shop, I'll catch y'all on the way back."

"Yeah, cool Dee, come by the Sugar Shack in Moses' garage. Hog Jaws and Lil Roamer took a nice string off today and want to cop some of that Acapulco gold. Some of the Slausonettes coming thru. Bird fixed the record player, you know he's good with his hands, and we having a lil get together for my birthday. Lafayette and Willie Woo bringing a few girls from the Westside, hope they don't start fighting." Bell laughed.

"Thanks but on second thought I'll get the smoke and drop it off. I have school in the morning."

"Righteous" was all Bell said.

Dandy pressed on and while crossing Florence Avenue could hear "So What", a composition by Miles, blowing from a loudspeaker on top of the record-shop. As soon as his foot stepped on the sidewalk, rays from a spotlight stymied his vision! Another staggering step triggered a boisterous command, "Freeze, another step and you're dead!"

13

Dandy's mind raced. The rollers! He always watched his back but apparently they had been watching too. If they found the weed in the lining of his coat he was surely gone. He wondered if he was snitched on or was it the usual harassment.

"Okay Mr. Dandy Dee, take that hat off and place your hands on top of your nappy head and get on your knees." The voice was familiar and so was the smell of the chewed up stogie cocked in Sgt. Baker's, aka Cowboy, mouth. "Let's go for a little ride pretty boy."

His sidekick slammed Dandy into the rear seat of the plain unmarked four door Ford with brute authority.

After a moment or two of silence, Cowboy broke the ice. "You're a smart kid Dandy. You don't put up any resistance. You don't scream police brutality and you haven't asked what this is all about, so keep it smart when I ask questions."

Dandy stared at the overweight cop with daggers in his eyes and remained silent.

The pock-faced partner hit the accelerator and sped off in the opposite direction of the 77th Street police station.

Dandy immediately became alarmed.

Cowboy took the floor, "Where are your fellow gang members Hog Jaws and Lil Roamer?"

Dandy said nothing.

"Don't play dumb with me. Thru my sources I know they're the ones who jacked the messenger from Martin's Department Store at ten thirty this morning. They will be caught and I want the collar."

Dandy was trembling inside but masked it perfectly and spoke, "If you know who did it why you harassing me? I ain't about no gang activity no more."

Cowboys wide grin revealed tobacco stained teeth as he spoke; "Now that's an understatement. You been keeping a low profile for a couple of years now but you still in the loop. You are very aware of goings on just the same."

Dandy countered, "I'm not eighteen yet. I don't know nothing and ain't got nothing to say. Book me if you want to but it's a waste of time."

"Have it your way punk, you're under arrest for aiding and abetting fugitives from a robbery, your brother can't come get you like he did for those curfew violations. The juvie authorities can house your ass until I catch your friends." He said bluffing.

Dandy held his mug calmly, he was rattled inside because of the weed but there was no way he would help the police under any circumstances. It was a code he grew up with.

The vice car made a U-turn and headed back towards the station. When they entered the interrogation room the cuffs were removed and the numbness subsided as the blood circulated.

"Take that coat and the rest of your clothing off." The snaggletooth jailer barked.

Cowboy reeled backwards on the heels of the cowboy boots that gave him his moniker, while lighting a fresh cigar and blowing the smoke in Dandy's face. "Have you changed your mind?"

"Hold your funky breath Cowboy, you know this is bogus and I don't know where the people are that you're looking for." Dandy replied sarcastically, and prayed the packages in the lining of his coat wouldn't be found.

The pock-faced cop patted Dandy down again and meticulously squeezed his shirt and pants. He then felt inside Dandy's shoes. He flipped the pockets of the maxi coat inside out and slid his palm along the lining.

Dandy knew he had a case when his hands stopped abruptly and he flashed a shitty smile while peering up with glee in his eyes. "Ah haa! What do we have here? You really are a dummy after all." He pulled out a switchblade and ripped the lining wide open where the packages of weed were exposed.

By now a blue suited audience had gathered. Several remarks were made, but Dandy didn't hear them, his mind was on Judge Miller, the judge who promised him some lock-up time if he ever saw him in his court again. This was when he and two of his homeboys, Squirt and Lil Bo, were falsely arrested for a theft three other kids did. When it was established that they weren't the guilty ones they were cut loose, but Miller, who was known as the hanging judge, issued a stern warning. The old geezer had once sent his own son to forestry camp for being incorrigible back in the day. He had also referred the young homeboy Silk to be tried as an adult for a murder he didn't commit. He wound up getting life and won't see daylight for some time.

***

True to his pattern, Judge Miller showed no mercy. "Dandy Dixon, for the crime of possession of marijuana and with the intent to sell I see no mitigating circumstances in this case, only a blatant disregard for the law; factors that outweigh your brother's plea for leniency. You are hereby ordered to be a ward of the state of California. Youth authority has a place for delinquents like your self. I hope that on your twenty-first birthday you

16

re-enter society a man with honorable and respectable intent for the law and join the legal workforce."

Cowboy snickered and said, "See you when you get back."

Tyrone yelled out an expletive phrase and had to be restrained. Freda cried with the boys as the drop of the gavel exploded like an atomic bomb.

He still prayed it was all a bad dream until the explosive slam of iron gates echoed through the corridors of the dual vocational institute serving as a rude awakening to his new reality.

Chapter 3

Paper Letters of Stone Foundation

Dandy adjusted after accepting full responsibility for his own errors and time took flight. The months flew by. Within sixteen months he had earned a gold certificate in welding and was studying blueprint reading. He could have earned a General Education Diploma but his plan was to enroll in adult school at night and walk across the stage for graduation and be presented with a diploma as his mother admonished him to do.

He worked out and read a great deal because someone had told him reading was knowledge and knowledge was power. He swore to never make another mistake. He grew tall and muscular, but most of all shrewd, ambitious, and cautious.

Quite a few guys from his old neighborhood came and a few went home, so he wasn't surprised when he saw a friend named Cartoon in a typing class.

He was trying to type a letter as Dandy cut in, "Hey what's up Toon?"

"Dandy?" He asked then stated, "Hey man I almost didn't recognize you. You're taller and buffed up off that iron. Looking good soldier."

"Yeah guess I was a late bloomer cause I shot straight up. I been growing and exercising since I got here, when did you check in?"

"I been here about two weeks and just hit the main population a few days ago."

They talked and got caught up with current events on the streets. Cartoon mentioned Hog Jaws and Lil Roamer finally getting caught for the robbery.

Dandy added, "Yeah I heard they got five to life and doing their bit in San Quentin and Lil Bo and Polly finally got married."

"Man! And Chief is a supervisor at the shipyard."

"Good to know, I'm going to look him up. I got welding skills now."

Toon then said, "Guess you heard about your boy Stanley killing his self over the lil dame that had his nose wide open enough for a freight train to drive up."

"Wow! I heard he did but didn't know why." Dandy proclaimed with sadness.

"Put the Hari Kari lick down over the girl named Crystal. Come to find out she was never his girl, and he was the only one who thought she was. Anyway, he kissed up to her all thru the senior year and when graduation came she went to the prom with Slim Dotson. She quit speaking to him and he couldn't handle it. He took a straight razor and wacked his throat from ear to ear two times in the back of his Pop's record shop. They said blood was gushing everywhere. He bled to death before the ambulance got there."

19

"Come on Toon! He didn't check out like that."

"Sad to say, but he did and that's the truth."

Dandy inquired, "What became of Crystal? And she had a friend named Priscilla, what happened to her?"

Toon replied, "Don't know what happened to Crystal, she vanished after Stanley passed. I didn't know Priscilla but I had seen her on campus. My sister Vicky mentioned that she went down south to attend some college they both wanted to go to but Priscilla came back a few months ago. I'll write Vicky and see if she can give her your hook up. Write your Y.A. number down."

Dandy's eyes began to sparkle as he spoke. "Thanks homey, I ain't heard from none of my old female friends since I been down."

"No big thing my brother" Toon asserted with a smile.

***

Three weeks later Priscilla appeared by way of pen and paper.

Dear Dandy,

I was overwhelmed when Crystal said you wanted me to write you. It's been some years and now I know why you didn't show up for the date we had. Too bad what happened to Stanley, but he told me and Crystal that you had to leave town and wasn't interested in being with us. It seemed a little odd at the time. I knew he was obsessed with my friend but I never dreamed he would go as far as he did. At any rate, I'm pleased to learn you had not forgotten me…I'm still curious about you now as the day me and Crystal were asking about you.

What are your plans when you are released? Tell me about yourself. Stanley said you only had interest in me and that's a good thing, right? But I'm pleased we have a connection and we shall see where the connection leads us.

Please write me at Crystal's address. The people I stay with might not want a letter from prison to come to their home. People are strange like that I don't want to stir up any controversy. Crystal will give me your letters and forward mine to you.

I enclosed twenty dollars, I'm sure anyone in prison can use some money. I intend to stay connected this time…Meanwhile, keep your chin up, hurry home, and remember all goodbyes ain't gone.

So long for now.

Priscilla

Dear Priscilla,

This brief letter is being sent with high hopes of catching you in the very best of health and wellbeing.

Your kite was a sweet surprise. I mean I wasn't expecting to hear from you so soon.

I hope that you can write on a regular basis because I'm not one of these convicts that stalk the mailman when mail call is announced. I'm not setting myself up for a disappointment if you don't respond in a timely

fashion. It makes the time harder to deal with. I prefer to do without the letters if you can't do that. I will still pay my regards when I rise up out of this modern day plantation, no hard feelings.

You're the only person I have received a letter from besides my family and it's a pure pleasure to hear from you. And hopefully we can build a solid foundation for a strong relationship. Let's proceed and see where the dominoes fall. Time tells all.

Now that that's been said. I'm well, considering the circumstances. It could be better, but it could be worse. Basically, I'm rolling with the punches and looking forward to better days when I hit the streets.

I plan on coping a job and a pad of my own, but we will see what happens.

Life is short and I hate I have to give these people some of my years, but on the flip side I'm young and ambitious. I have no doubt that I'll bounce back stronger than ever.

What about you? How you living and what plans and goals do you have?

Sit your fine self down now and share your thoughts. I will definitely respond.

Meanwhile, be good to yourself and let's pick up where we left off mystery lady that day when I first met you and Crystal.

With Sincerity,

Dandy

***

About a week later, and every week thereafter, Dandy received a letter from Priscilla. The communication was consistent and blossomed into a compatible and very promising relationship.

Chapter 4

To "P" or Not To "P"

A little over three years produced a lot of changes. Dandy thought as the forty-nine maple flowed thru the thick of the Village up San Pedro St. It appeared to have aged thirty years as opposed to nearly four.

Burnt down and abandoned structures reflected the aftermath of the Watts Rebellion in '65. Dandy lit off the bus several stops before the exit at he and his brother's block. He didn't mind the walk, he actually wanted to. He wanted to feel the neighborhood again and let the good and the bad soak in.

His confinement produced a clear point of vision he had never paid a lot of attention to growing up. Singing, laughter, lovemaking, cursing, swearing, fussing, and fighting were all toned down by the sound of music blowing from doorways and windows. The blues, jazz, doo whoop and soul.

Craig's Diner engulfed the air with the succulent aroma of hickory-smoked barbeque, temporarily overpowering the stench of gutters. Elder seniors were bent over barely getting along, as drunks, drug addicts and hustlers tried to get thru another day.

He also noted young children skipping along in a carefree world. Girls jumped rope and practiced dance steps. Boys played marbles and shot hoops on the blacktop. Church people sang their troubles away for the moment, never missing a note or a beat as the fruit man boasted about the freshest fruit in town from a loudspeaker on top of his slow moving truck.

The buildings had stressful expressions but birds of the Village glided above chirping with glee. When exhaust fumes settled down the sweet smell of garden flowers dominated the atmosphere. The highs and lows of home were a welcome experience. Walking down the residential block towards home which were owned by most of its inhabitants Dandy noted some that were well manicured and maintained and some in need of a facelift. He reflected on what Schoolboy always preached, "A brand-new car will loose value when you drive it off the showroom floor. Buy a house and it will gain value with each passing year."

Sweetmeat and his constituents were still caught up in the viscous web of despair and bad habits, but young kids caravanned to and from the elementary school on 66th St. with high hopes and ambitions.

Home was mellow madness and sweet misery, accompanied by a feeling of comfort and security amid familiar surroundings. Nonetheless, he knew that one day he would take flight and leave what has always been home. He loved the people in the Village and vowed to never forget his roots. As bad as he wanted to help the people he knew he had to help himself first.

Dandy felt like a celebrity when Freda, his brother, the boys and his niece Fatima, the latest addition to the family, swarmed him with hugs, kisses, and endless 'welcome homes'. After his favorite meal of fried fish, potato salad, collard greens, macaroni and cheese with hush puppies on the side he thought he wouldn't eat for another week. But the Johnson's from next door brought a pineapple upside down cake, a tray of peach cobbler, and a pot of smothered chicken. He had to remind himself that he is supposed to eat to live…not live to eat.

Tyrone broke out a rare bottle of Piper Heidsieck Rose wine that he found in the basement years ago.

They drank to freedom.

Tyrone began, "Dandy boy, I hope you stay home this time. This is as much yours as it is mines. MaDear stressed the importance of family and unity and keeping our property. She had the house Homesteaded and wrote in her will that the house is to be handed down to each generation. It's not a huge mansion but it's home, as she would say. And if we ever wanted to move off the eastside we could but we would have to rent it out and divide the income. We just had to keep the land."

Tyrone took a sip as he continued "Most of our people, originally from the South, migrated to this village from other parts of the Eastside along Central Avenue in pursuit of jobs and a better life. Hard working people that got jobs and bought homes here when employment was fruitful. They also had skills. Remember Mr. Dutton, the TV repairman and Mr. Kennedy that had the fix it shop? And the Grey Brothers auto shop on San Pedro, along with a lot of other stores. Big business and corporations slowly snuffed them out and the chance for us to maintain what they started."

"Yeah, that's what MaDear, Daddy, School, and most of the elders believed in. And they diligently paid those coins on life insurance policies. On a few occasions when she didn't have it she would tell me to go to the door and tell the insurance man she wasn't home and to come back the next day, and she would have it the next day." Dandy chuckled and they both laughed.

Tyrone continued, "I hope you have plans for a career and a family now that you're twenty-one. Don't you agree?"

"Yeah Ty, I've had a lot of time to ponder the future and I don't have all the fine details laid out just yet, but while walking home I thought about coping a little bachelor pad and get this welding job at the shipyard. Chief is a foreman down there."

Tyrone looked off in another direction of the room and confessed, "Lil brother, there is a small problem with that."

Curiously Dandy asked, "What do you mean?"

"I had to use some of your money you left here." But quickly added, "My income tax return will be here any day now. Things got a little tight when Fatima came on the set. I even had to use some of your money to send to you when I did." He humbly waited to read an expression on his brother's face.

With calmness Dandy said, "That's cool big brah, you would have not used it if it wasn't necessary. You been looking out for me before MaDear passed. It ain't nothing but some money. And it ain't like we can't go get no more."

"Thanks Dandy, I didn't want to say anything and just replace it when my check comes."

"Don't give it a second thought. Forget about paying the shorts back."

They smiled at each other and it turned into laughter as they had another drink and yet another.

Dandy was awakened by the smell of fresh baked biscuits and the sound of eggs sizzling in a skillet. Freda may have lost her hourglass figure years ago but her skills in the kitchen were superb.

With a full stomach and a hot shower he pondered his next move. Well Dandy he thought to his self, I've outgrown a lot of old ways and my clothes also. I'll see if Tyrone can loan me something to wear before I take a stroll.

Walking down San Pedro he knew he couldn't recapture lost time but he hoped to make up for it. Opening Schoolboy's door he was greeted with handshakes and "welcome home's" by four or five local gamblers. One such gambler by the moniker "Bet All Bill", a friend of Mr. Dixon, had a good night at the card house on Central Avenue and slid a fifty dollar bill into his pocket and voiced, "Here's a little something to keep the jinx off you son."

Schoolboy added, "Don't spend it all in one place and if you lay a bet with it make sure it's a cinch tab winner. And that's hard to do unless you got Abe in your boson, a stacked deck, or T's in your pocket!"

The house roared with laughter as they made their exit.

Schoolboy went to his table that served as a desk and asked, "How about a taste of good Scotch?"

Dandy quickly said, "No thanks School, I had my share last night. I'm really not a drinker."

"Good reasoning," School said and added. "Everything good to you ain't necessarily good for you. You like a son to me Dandy and it would give me great pleasure to see you make it in life. Your stay may have been for the best cause Bell and several of your old friends are hooked on **smack**, which don't make em real bad guys…. It's the dog already in some of them that it brings out so well. The way it drives them. It's the chase for the drug that puts wear and tear on them rather than the drug itself…that 'monkey' is a heavy load to carry and feed. Anyway, you missed that era that snagged them. I said all that to say this; there's no need to look them up unless you want to join them. I know you want to catch up with things, but some things are better off left alone."

Dandy nodded in agreement and listened as school continued.

"I can't tell you what to do because ultimately you're going to do what you want to do anyway, but let the record reflect that Ole School told you. The stage ain't changed, just the people. After high school most of your associates got drafted or enlisted in Vietnam. Some became Black Panthers or other militant groups; still others hit the streets to be hustlers or players. A few got married and settled down with jobs at Goodyear, Firestone, the shipyards or aircraft factories. Some continued their education and are about to become doctors and lawyers. A lot are in prison, as you know. The Panthers did a lot for the community. They had a breakfast program for the under privileged kids all over town. They even started Swahili classes to help teach self -identity. I gave my support and dropped donations here and there. Some of your homeboys are Muslims. I don't know a lot about the religion but they are always dressed clean and appear to be very dignified. I buy bean pies from them all the time. Now there it is, you can take off from where you were when you left or you can elevate yourself up and out of these slums. Whatever you do, do it well and don't allow it to do you. Never compromise your convictions son, if you sweep floors or become a brain surgeon. Do it well."

With old but strong hands School gave him a c-note. "Add that to your bank. "

Dandy spoke, "Thanks School, not just for the ends but the wisdom as well."

School's serious face smiled and asked, "Question, have you bestowed some fine tender with that load you been holding?"

"Not yet" Dandy stated and grinned.

"Well be selective, a lot of things are easy to catch but hard to get rid of." School warned.

Dandy left, but School's voice resonated with him. He was like a father and his advice was always sound, real and unfiltered.

***

Dandy hopped on the Forty-Nine Maple and rode downtown. He bought a pair of slacks and a colorful shirt to match. He came home, showered again and got dressed.

Priscilla's address was on the west side of town. The West side was a more upscale area but it had its ghettos here and there like the East side and Dee was surprised to see Priscilla's pad was located in the more plush section of the west side.

"Is this Miss Parker's residence? This is Dandy Dixon calling." His voice echoed in the speaker box located outside the apartment complex. Several seconds passed before a voice spoke.

"Who did you say was calling?"

He didn't like repeating himself and sarcastically said, "This is Dandy Dixon."

Again there was hesitation.

Just as he thought about leaving a buzzer went off and the main entrance popped open. Number nine was upstairs and as he stepped up the stairs he thought to himself, Now this is a jazzy layout, never seen a pool in the middle of a courtyard before. I wonder if the interior is just as nice?

The door opened and a beautiful young woman smiled with the same 'frosting on the cake' as the curvaceous young girl he had seen in high school.

She broke the stare by saying, "Well please come in," and led him to a red velvet love seat.

Dandy stated, "You sounded as though you were busy or something."

"No not at all. I wasn't expecting you so soon. Crystal mentioned you getting out but didn't say when."

Curious, Dandy inquired, "Didn't you get my letter?"

"Letter?", was all she asked and continued, "I'm slightly confused but why let it worry us." She leaned to his lips and planted a short but passionate kiss and then said, "Welcome home Dandy, you have really matured from a cute boy to a very handsome man."

He had never heard a personal compliment like that and blushed slightly. Not to be outdone he stole a line from an old black and white movie he had seen several years in the past. With a charming smile that had confidence plastered all over it he countered, "I see nature has smiled on you as well." He chalked her confusion up to Crystal not giving her his last letter.

The day evolved into evening as they talked and became more acquainted. He thought about Crystal but didn't bring her up since things were moving along so smoothly. They had a toast of champagne and a puff of cannabis

31

then continued talking about how life had been for her, but something seemed to be missing. He couldn't pin point it, but he didn't give it any more thought either.

Smokey crooned romantic lyrics as they danced cheek to cheek in the middle of the living room floor. Dandy's heart thumped as his nature throbbed. Her heart quickened and her breathing accelerated as they stumbled into the bedroom. At the touch of penetrating her garden he released over three years of frustration. Embarrassment overcame him, but instantly vanished. His rejuvenated young body moved smoothly as he took charge and navigated with perfect balance within his lover. They loved slow, fast, hot and hard until succulent sounds of wet bodies engulfed the room. The explosions were repetitious and never seemed to end. They loved as neither had loved before.

Days passed and Dandy found himself still in Priscilla's apartment. This was a new phase of life for him and he was soaking it all up and enjoying every bit of it. Priscilla worked nights and cared for him during the day. She bought him clothes and didn't want him to look for work, not yet anyway.

One Sunday morning he laid in bed watching football as Priscilla prepared breakfast. All the treatment he was receiving was sweet, but he needed breathing room. He began to feel sheltered and possessed. His thoughts were broken off by the ring of the telephone on the nightstand next to him. Once, twice, three times. Just as the fourth ring sounded he lifted the receiver off the hook.

Priscilla grabbed the wall phone in the kitchen at the same time and said "Hello."

A soft voice inquired, "Good morning were you asleep?"

"No, I was fixing breakfast for Dandy."

The voice asked, "How is he girl, has he changed much? I haven't heard from you in awhile and decided to call and see about visiting when you two have time."

"He is very fine, and packing too!" Priscilla boasted in a cold voice. "It seems he is all you are really interested in. Don't come by today or any other day."

Tears came to Crystal's eyes but her voice concealed it. "I cannot believe your attitude. Or allowing anyone to come between our friendship. Are you serious?"

"Dead serious." Priscilla assured, "I know how you feel about Dandy and I don't intend to lose him."

Crystal felt betrayed and reminded her, "What's come over you, sure I was attracted to him, we both were but he preferred you. I'm the one who wrote him for you because you said you didn't have the time. You didn't care so much when he was away, but I cared so much for both of you, which turned out to be me caring too much!" Her voice began to tremble and tears were already rolling so she saved face by hanging up.

Dandy thumbed thru Priscilla's phone book and wrote down Crystal's phone number. He jumped into the shower, then darted out and got dressed. Then grabbed the keys to Priscilla's Mustang.

"Daddy! Where are you going? Your breakfast is ready."

"Keep it warm, I'll be right back."

At the first phone booth he came to a screeching halt. He dialed the number he wrote on a matchbook cover and was greeted by an elderly voice, "Hello, Jones residence."

He returned with, "Hello, and how are you? May I speak to Crystal?"

In a few seconds a sharp, angry voice blasted out, "Hello who is this?"

Dandy answered, "Don't sound so mean, you're too pretty for that tone of voice."

Again she said in a softer voice, "Who is this?"

"This is Dandy Dixon."

Her breath got short and she became speechless…He continued, "Crystal, I have to talk with you, can we meet?"

A moment of silence passed before she asked, "Where?"

He replied, "Anywhere, I don't care."

"Okay, I'll be at the coffee shop on Manchester and La Brea in thirty minutes." She confirmed.

She walked as graceful as the first day he laid eyes on her. She was looking around the coffee shop but he wanted to relish the moment as he observed her from a distance. She was radiantly beautiful without any makeup; just a modest, almost homely dressed sister.

Their eyes met and she rushed to the table in the back corner of the shop. She sat down before he could pull her chair out and spoke, "I was wondering if I would recognize you. You look well. More mature, but you still have that young schoolboy look. How have you been?"

"Thank you Crystal, you're still adorable. I'm fair, just getting used to this so-called freedom and getting set to put a plan in order. How has life been treating you?"

She replied, "Not bad at all, I'm working at General Hospital and going to college at night. What did you want to talk about?"

He unraveled the mystery with six words; "I overheard your call this morning."

"Oh I see." She said and shyly gazed out at traffic thru a picture window.

Dandy asked, "Why did you write those letters and sign them from Priscilla?"

Still gazing outside she confessed, "For several reasons. I was already corresponding with someone else in prison and didn't want to be labeled a letter groupie. It was nothing serious. Then Stanley had told Priscilla and myself that you only wanted to talk to her when we met. And when Cartoon's sister Vicky told me you wanted to get in touch I assumed you wanted to write Priscilla. I told her but she didn't want to write you. She said she would if she had time, and I didn't want you to be disappointed, so I wrote for her. I actually told her I was, but she always seemed unfazed."

Dandy asked, "So was it love for me or for her that made you write."

She answered, "Well her as a friend, and you I can't explain."

"Now I'm seeing things more clearly. Let me set something straight. It may have been a schoolboy crush but you couldn't have told me I wasn't in love with you at first sight. Stanley told me you were his girl and your friend wanted to meet me. I ain't gonna lie. You both were attractive in different ways to me. But I went along with plans for a date with her because I wanted to be close to you."

She expressed herself candidly, "Life is a trip." She sighed and looked deep inside his eyes.

Dandy placed his chin in his palm and leaned closer to her.

"I saw you that first day of school too. And when you couldn't get in my class I was sad and was wondering why. So I can't say it was love at first sight as you stated. But, I did then and right now have butterflies in my stomach. My heart is fluttering and the average girl would hold such secrets near and dear to her heart, but I'm not your average girl. But things are already written on the wall and everything happens for a reason. You and Priscilla are hooked up according to her."

Dandy declared, "If I leave Priscilla would you embrace me and be my woman?"

"I can't do that Dandy. She definitely has a thing for you and I don't want to come between that happiness. She is still a friend despite her actions."

"I really don't agree." He stated with confusion. "She didn't care about your feelings." He added.

She answered, "You probably don't, it's a sister thing. I don't have enough malice in my heart to hurt her."

"I think your feelings for her are stronger than your feelings for me. I will cut her loose and be your man right now."

A grey film came over her face as she contemplated. Solemnly she said "No."

Although his knees slightly buckled, Dandy still sat erect and tugged his collar, "Alright, I just wanted the whole story, now that you have rejected me there is nothing else to say."

Crystal was torn, "Don't say it like that, please."

"It comes out the same however I say it.... Take care of yourself and be good to yourself. Maybe all goodbye's won't be gone one day!"

She smiled at the quote from her letter and said, "I better go now, I need to do some thinking and please don't tell Priscilla about our conversation."

"I won't". He assured and asked, "Can I drop you off?"

"No, I have a way."

It hurt both of them to depart and the thought of never seeing each other again was even more painful.

As suddenly as Crystal had come into his life, she was gone. His feelings were crushed and he wondered if the weird hurting sensation he was feeling in his heart was what they called love. If so, he vowed to never ever again in life to be hurt like the hurt he was feeling. He could love a woman in the future but he would never again be 'in love' with a woman. Love at first sight must be a reality. One he would never put feelings into again. He was devastated, but not destroyed.

He took a deep breath and gathered his composure. He dismissed Crystal from his mind and rationalized that once upon a time he never knew her.

***

Dandy and Priscilla resumed there relationship and he never brought up Crystal's name, although he couldn't shake the thought of her. Weeks passed and the thrill became old and barely existed. He thought of making it on his own. He located his homeboy Chief, but the shipyard had a hiring freeze. For a couple more weeks he sought a job to no avail.

He just couldn't see a future in the menial jobs he was offered and when he applied for the job of his skill…."You don't have enough on the job experience", "You're too young", "We forgot to take the help sign down", or "Sorry" were the responses he received. His frustration swelled and Priscilla was an outlet for him.

She sat on a pillow in the living room next to where Dandy was stretched out by the stereo listening to The Blue Notes. "What's wrong Dee? You haven't spoken over a dozen words in the last couple of days, and when you did it was 'Will you leave me alone Priscilla', or ' Be quiet Priscilla', she stated.

"I have things on my mind Priscilla, every so often a man has a need for deep reflective thought, so give me some space!" he demanded.

Priscilla's guilt mounted and Dandy's strange actions led her to believe that someone may have told him the secret she kept from him. She was silent for several minutes as she plotted. I wish I knew how he will react… oh well, I'll work up a tear and put my sympathy mask on, with glossy eyes she began, "Daddy, I need to talk to you."

"Not now you don't," he barked.

"Yes I do." She confessed and continued, "I hid something from you but I can't conceal it any longer."

Dandy rolled over to face her and waited for her next words.

She faked a sniffle and lowered her head as she began, "I don't go to a factory at night and the weekend work is not overtime. I go to Hollywood. I'm a 'Lady of the Evening', ' a Sporting Girl', a prostitute. That's how I survive." By now she was close to a scream as tears rolled down her cheeks. "I would have told you sooner but I was afraid I would loose you." She scanned his face for a sign or a reaction, but he was like a pillar of stone. She continued with a cracked voice, "I love you baby, there is five thousand dollars in my savings, it's all for you. Every time I sold myself it was for you. Will you please accept me as your lady? I'll die being loyal to you. Pretty please with money stacked on top!"

Dandy stood erect and silently walked to the closet and put his topcoat on and stepped out the front door. "I'll talk to you when I get back." Was all he said, with ice in his voice.

"Dam" she said out loud. What is he thinking, what is he going to do? Oh God, did I do the wrong thing? She questioned her self.

Dandy zipped through traffic by reflex; his mind was on Priscilla and what his next move was. The truth she spit out was shocking and painful too because he did have feelings for her. Should he leave, or accept her offer? If he did, pimping wasn't his forte. These indecisions swirled around his brain like a hurricane…continuously until his mind locked on him. He knew the Old Master had the key.

After hearing the whole story, the elder with a silver grey process and smooth skin for a man in his late fifties leaned back in his chair. He stroked his neatly trimmed goatee with one hand and clutched his pipe in the other while gazing upward in thought.

Dandy observed his gestures.

Schoolboy was clad in a midnight blue suit; a powder blue hand crafted knit turtle neck sweater and a pair of Bannister dress shoes. He sported a wafer thin solid gold watch with diamonds that sparkled when he sat up and placed both palms in prayer position and spoke, "Sounds to me that you have to make a decision before we know what choice to make. Do you want to keep Priscilla?"

"Yes, but I'm no pimp." He stated.

School advised, "Now that she revealed herself you have to be one. If not leave her alone." School grinned and continued, " You started pimping the day you were born. Now pimping is a dirty word now a days so refer to your self as a 'gentleman of leisure', or a 'Mack'. Hell, babies come in the world doing it. The president and governments do it. Dogs, cats, and other pets as well. They don't know it and they frown on the word but listen to the School. Priscilla is a sporting lady and you just so happened to be at the right time and place in her life when she wanted to choose a man. It was just the luck of the draw. I experienced something similar in my youth. I was ditching school because I was fascinated with the fast life, vice, and the glitz n' glamour. A madam of several houses of ill repute, whorehouses, to be specific, caught me in my teenage years. She was around fifty and scooped me up and took swell care of me. I wasn't allowed to work or do anything but tell her what I wanted. When she died she left me three houses, cash, jewelry, and several insurance policies. The rest is history. I don't need this business, I just love the life and being in the mix. You probably didn't know it but Sweetmeat was a bonafide player in his day."

"I thought he was something like that. He always tells me that all the elderly women in the neighborhood love Sweetmeat. I occasionally see him at night creeping around. Slipping in and out of back doors with a grin." Dandy agreed.

"All that's true. His lady was Big Angie. She was the baddest booster on the West Coast. Unfortunately she was killed in a car accident several years ago and he's been going down like the Titanic ever since." School added and continued, "Back to Priscilla, she has been doing well on her own but probably knew a day would come where she would have to choose a man. I'm sure she's a target on some pimp's radar. But she's sharp. She was priming you to be more than a sex partner after y'all first got together. Resting and dressing you. She's sincere cause dames like her are more devoted to one man than most housewives. You have to know and primarily understand that when she lays her body down with 'Trick Willie' her mind is on you. It's just business, so don't allow your emotions to creep into your game. No, never let emotions control you. That can be disastrous. It's like everything in life...Balance is the key. You show feelings in certain situations and in most others you don't.

40

She is seeking security and as long as you provide it she will be stable with her role. Normally a guy has to shine to get chosen, but you just got lucky. Everyone can't be a player. You didn't know her but I'm sure you heard the legend of "Coup de Ville."

Dandy nodded in full attention and School continued, "She bought her man "Pretty Dog" a brand spanking new Cadillac every single solitary year for at least twenty years until she passed last year. And Dog was just that to her, a dog. But it was something about the dog in him that she liked. And he looked like the creature from the black lagoon. I couldn't figure it out and a wise man once told me that a man will wind up in the nut house or the cemetery trying to figure out why a woman does certain things. I know cats that married their best working woman and raised a family and lived happily ever after. They were far and few in between but all kinds of hands get dealt in life…Play yours and get what you can out of her. The sporting life is like a merry-go-round and as fast as they jump on, they jump off just as fast. So take what you got coming while it's available. Be hard and a tower of strength. Be a man about yourself at all times. You are the director and you call all the shots. Some players disagree but I say let her have a right to an opinion or express one…listen to her if it's done in private at the proper time and place, not a crowd. Remember the balance."

School took a swig of ice water and wiped his mouth with the back of his hand and resumed, "Just be a man at all times, if you slip or show any sign of weakness she will loose all respect and drop you like a bad habit. And run all over you like she should. A woman will tolerate a lot of flaws in a man but if love or respect are gone, so is she. She may violate one of your rules at times, she just be checking to see if you're still the same man you were when she got with you. It's all fair son because things generally end the way they begin. Now if you are serious, remember the game will only be as good to you as you are to it. If you're going to be a pimp, a welder, or a janitor do it well, it ain't what you do, its how you do it."

41

Dandy looked into School's eyes and declared, "I'm going to see where all this leads to School. I love you man like a father and appreciate the guidance."

"Ain't no thang. Game is to be sold, not told, but you a special exception son." School said and continued, "Now that you're a gentleman you have to walk it, talk it, and be about it. Get your hair laid in a Kennedy Swoop at the process shop on Broadway. Be known as 'Dandy Dee' or 'Double Dee' and develop your own unique style. First thing you do is walk into the door and tell her to put some clothes on, we going to the bank. Get your money she got saved for you. You can hold your own better than anyone on the planet. Then send her to work and get ready for the headaches." School flashed a grin and asserted, "Me and no one else can make you a pimp. You have to have it in you. Follow the guidelines and get your feet wet. The game has to be lived and learned. Iceberg left a dam good blueprint but this is dam near Nineteen-Seventy. Men are going to the moon, and although the game remains the same, new twists and innovations are presented all the time."

Dandy took a deep breath and released it with words, "I hope I can remember all you said, how do you know all these things School?"

School just smiled and said, "I'll be here if you need me…God willing that is. I'm not a lettered man. I missed the reading and writing coming up but I was gifted with the sharp ability to look and observe my surroundings, I listen and hear very well, I can read in between the lines of unspoken words. I'm long in the tooth and been attentive all my life. Now go handle your business."

Chapter 5

Rolling With A Gangster Lean and Shattered Dreams

D andy Dee, as he became better known took to the life like a baby duck to the pond. He played it by ear and learned fast. When Priscilla tried to tell him how to act and react, he cut her off and pretended he already knew. He managed his money well and on a cool December night in Nineteen Sixty-Nine he and Priscilla cut thru traffic in a Pearl White Brougham with burgundy interior fresh off the showroom floor. He was laid in a tailor-made burgundy leisure suit with white stitching and a white Fedora on his crown. He turned the temperature control down a notch and smiled to his self. Six months had produced the new Dandy Dixon. Priscilla had a bust free run, but he wondered how much longer her luck would last. He secured a bondsman and a fixer lawyer that he hoped to never use.

She couldn't take her eyes off him. He was so cold, calm, and fly. She was proud to be the main woman of the new face on the set, the only woman he would have if she had it her way. She didn't want to share, but knew that day was coming.

Dandy immediately gained respect amongst his peers and the eyes of other ladies of the evening. Dandy broke the silence as he turned down Broadway. "When you date a trick remember to get a number and give the answering service number out. I want you to build your book so you don't have to deal with these streets. Do you understand?"

"Yes I do Daddy, I been trying but most of my regulars can't afford for me to call their homes, you know," she said with a calm tone.

"I always understand. But you can get a buddy's number, their local bar, or their job. Encourage them to leave messages at the answer service with some kind of contact. Start thinking. This is for our longevity. I don't want to stay on this level all our life. I'm going to the top and want my Queen with me." He reached back and grabbed her hand, squeezed it gently and further declared, "That position is yours but if you lag, you loose."

"I'm qualified Daddy and will prove myself." She assured him.

He parked in back of the Five Four Ballroom and spoke, "Be careful and handle my business." He patted her on her rear end as she climbed out the back seat of the Cadillac.

Just then a hooker named Star approached the car and spoke, "Hey Mr. Dandy, how you doing handsome?"

Before another word could be uttered Priscilla sharply intervened, "How is it out here tonight? It must be slow cause you ain't got no money in your hand to approach my man with before speaking, Sugar."

"It is rather slow," she muttered slowly.

Like clockwork, Priscilla's tongue lashed out. "You ain't broke luck yet and the track is this way" as she pulled her arm towards the streets.

Dandy was cracking up on the inside as he cranked the "Hog" up and peeled rubber onto the streets. He was getting ready to recruit a stable and it was going to be interesting to see how Priscilla would adapt and hold it down.

Slauson and Broadway was lit up like a Christmas tree and the night looked prosperous. Tricks and hoes ducked around corners and jumped into doorways when the black and white or vice cars rolled by on patrol. It reminded Dandy of musical chairs. When they passed the ladies of the evening emerged from sidewalk cracks and everywhere else patting wigs back in place, resuming their most sensual positions and beckoning or waving to potential customers. Then right back into hiding when a warning call broadcasted five o's return.

Dandy swung off Slauson and onto the Harbor Freeway. He took the northbound lane and stomped the accelerator; the big machine squatted down and the Vogues gripped the asphalt with authority. It mellowed into traffic and the suspension smoothly glided up and down in perfect rhythm to the sound of Horace Silvers musical tribute to his father.

Dandy was relishing the good life, or so it appeared, and nearly forgot that the test of bad days can emerge at any time. Good days and bad days are both a test of patience; the reward can be for you or against you, depending on how you deal with it.

In twenty minutes he was on Sunset Boulevard in the heart of Hollywood. The Hog wheeled into the driveway entrance of the Players Paradise Club and Lounge. It was packed and the valet was besieged with parking luxury vehicles. "Be careful my man, you're under a lot of car here." Dandy warned.

"Yes sir, this is what I do." The valet said smiling.

The Players Paradise was home base for most players in the region, and out of towners. Pimps and hustlers of all degrees along with a faithful host of movie personalities and entertainment buffs frequented the club. There were a handful of after hour joints in town but this was the place to be before two AM. The band that normally would be rocking the atmosphere was on break. The bar overflowed with customers and waitress' carting drinks on trays.

Dandy moved past the traffic toward the Recreation Lounge located upstairs where he saw a few of his crowd. A Mack out of Oakland named Speedy Brown held the floor to a captivated audience. "So I tell the Filly to make me know it's too hot tonight on the track! Make your feet look like deer hoofs, just get my money. Get busted trying, why you think I have bondsmen all over the county, you'll be out in an hour!"

A young player named Sugar Cane cracked in fun, "See there Speedy, I always knew you were a sucker and getting soft. I know the dame and she ain't never made twenty dollars over bail money!"

The entire upper lounge roared and so did Speedy as he countered "You should know her. You kept her before me for six months!"

Again the house cracked up uncontrollably. After the chuckles settled down a good friend of Dandy's named Baby Talk asked in a high pitched voice, "What you drinking Double Dee?"

"Just a virgin long island tea for me, and thanks partner."

Talk raised his hand and snapped his finger to get the bartender's attention. "Bring a long island ice tea on the virgin side and a scotch with the white lady in it."

Patty, the white female bartender, blushed slightly and yelled out, "One virgin long island and one scotch and milk coming up."

The conversation flowed, most of it being how one's game was, how much money was clocked on a given night, or new game in the stable and ladies who left making room for fresh ones. Discreetly cocaine made the party rounds but Dandy passed. He wasn't a big drinker and might hit a joint every now and then but refrained from the blow ninety-nine percent of the time.

Shortly afterwards Dandy was told he had a phone call on the house phone. He got up and made it behind the bar. "Yeah, Dandy here."

A familiar, proper speaking voice relayed, "Priscilla just called. She's in the Newton Street sub station en route to Sybil Brand with a soliciting charge."

"Well raise her Mr. Cameron," Dandy snapped.

"The papers are already in order, just wanted your approval as instructed by you." The bondsman voiced.

"Right. You have the money and I'll have her come sign the papers first thing in the morning." Dandy promised.

"She will be back on the streets within an hour." Cameron assured.

While driving home Dandy reminded himself that he needed to gather that stable for a back-up during times like this.

Dandy sat at home waiting on Priscilla. This was her first bust and he needed to know how it went down so that he could figure out if it could be prevented in the future, or was it just one of the hazards of the game.

After five long hours Priscilla's key finally opened the door. She entered with a skinny-legged brown skinned hooker with a mini skirt and Ho Boots on. "Hi Daddy, I didn't come straight home because I wanted to bring some kind of money so I went to the stroll in Long Beach. This is Duchess, she got out the same time I did. She wants to be family and I had to set a good example. I knocked off a bill-fifty in a few hours and she made a hundred."

Dandy jumped into her face and snarled in a loud and vicious tone, "Don't ever change your location without notification. I must know where you are at all times. I worry about you, my business, and don't ever in life want to be guessing where my business is." His huge hands grabbed the back of her neck, pulling her right in front of his mug, within kissing distance and whispered, "Am I understood?" and turned to stare at Duchess' stunned face, "I'm talking to you too 'new boodie'."

They both nodded in agreement and promised, "Yes Sir Daddy."

Some players exercised physical abuse in certain situations, but this wasn't one such occasion for Dandy. He swore not to ever hit his women with closed fists. If it ever came to that, it was curtains and over between them. His style was patterned after a Smooth Mack not a Gorilla Mack.

"I'm sorry and please forgive me. I was so mad about the bust and didn't want to come home empty handed that's why I didn't think to call you." Priscilla begged.

"Just don't let it happen again. Show Duchess to the bathroom, give her some towels and whatever else she needs." Looking Duchess up and down he spoke, "When you're done come into my den and we'll have a talk." Dandy instructed.

She was from the mid-West and had come to Hollywood with high hopes of modeling. And soon found out how fast and hard dreams die. She was a fair looking dame with a slight stutter to her speech. No wonder Priscilla brought her home. She didn't feel like she was any sort of threat to her position, just a helping hand. Duchess was twenty years old and immature. She had been robbed and slapped around and knew she needed a man to protect and represent her if she chose to work the streets. She also knew it came with a price.

***

Dandy's name was really ringing off the hook. His ride, his jewelry, and dress really paid dividends. At the end of the year his stable was five deep with the addition of Carmen, Goldie, and Cherrie, the newest member of his royal family.

Dandy dropped into the club one night and was heckled by a few of his peers. When he stepped into the upper lounge Fast Eddie, Hollywood, and Diamond Shorty pretended not to see him…"Naw man, Dandy is a boss player, he don't do no free freaking and not get paid!" Declared Hollywood.

"Well I thought so too cause square broads can't pay like sporting ladies," Fast asserted.

"Maybe he's trying to turn square girls out. Then again, I knew an old washed up pimp named Silver who called it Sex Charging when he got busted with a square."

Just then they acted as if they were just seeing Dandy, "Kill all game," Fast chuckled and added, "Hey Dandy, we didn't see you partner."

"Yeah right. Now what's all the ribbing about?" Dandy demanded.

"You tell us ole buddy of ours. She's cute but definitely homely, green, and twice as square as a pool table," as he pointed to the far side of the room. "She's been waiting on you player."

Dandy smiled and said, "You lames better not be pulling my leg."

Crystal was enjoying the music and never saw him coming. He tapped her on the shoulder and smiled when she turned to face him, then said, "Let's go where we can talk."

49

She was startled at first but broke into a relieving smile when she gazed into his eyes and said, "Sure, I would like to have a word with you."

Dandy found a secluded spot and once they were seated he spoke, "How have you been beautiful?"

Crystal tried to conceal a worried disposition with a forced smile, "I'm getting by financially, but mentally it has been a challenge. My mother passed a month ago and I'm still dealing with it. We were very close. It was cardiac arrest, suddenly without a hint of warning."

"I share your grief and pray she has a peaceful journey. My deepest condolences to you and your family." Dandy delivered and added, "Life must continue Crystal."

Crystal replied, "I realize that, I'm twenty-two now and it took her passing for me to seriously focus on the shortness of life. Our entire future often lies in uncertainty, unless a plan is initiated. I'm at a dire juncture of my life. And I'm here to tell you that I want to start a family and share my dreams with you."

Dandy's eyes blew up like balloons. He sat there with his mouth gaped open trying to speak. Before he could spit out a word she continued, "I hope my forwardness isn't a turn off but I had to get it out and be frank with you. I can't explain why, but you are the only man I feel I could dedicate my life to. My heart speaks louder than my mouth."

Dandy formed his mouth to speak but she intervened, "Let me finish while it's able to come out. I have heard all about you and Priscilla's lifestyle. I don't care about that, my concern is our future. This life has no tomorrows for you Dandy, what happens when the women and the thrill are gone? I'll work until you can find a job. For some strange reason I love you. I tried to throw a blanket over my feelings but they keep coming back. I've dated other men but they left a hole in my heart."

Dandy looked at her with lines across his forehead and a perplexed expression. "Crystal, I can't deny my feelings toward you either. I mean it all sounds good, but the truth is I'm not giving up the life I live and love. We could have become a reality when I first came home but you didn't want to offend your friend. If you really had feelings for me then they were put on the back burner and you wanted me to accept your choice. This is unreal. Dam sho ain't fair. If we were to have a meeting of the minds it would be on my terms, not yours. The fast life ain't for you and I'm not about to give up these diamonds and the glitter. I'm having things in life that I want. Life is short, and sweet too if you make it that way. While I'm traveling thru it I want my trip to be as comfortable as possible and secure as possible. This is a dog eat dog world where the big eat the little. So I'm gaining ground to fight on and stay alive. It's a capitalistic society and I'm getting down for mine. You and I can't gain anything on a square level living paycheck to paycheck."

"Maybe we wouldn't, but we can have love, peace of mind and be content knowing the bills will get paid every month." Crystal confessed.

Dandy delivered the ultimatum, "My mind could never be at peace if I was broke. And living just to exist is not a peaceful situation that I desire. I couldn't love you or myself, I definitely wouldn't be happy. So if you're not coming into my world on my terms then we're wasting each other's time."

She cast a long piercing look deep into his eyes and prophesied, "When the illusion is gone I intend on being here waiting for you." She stood up and briskly walked towards the exit.

Dandy wondered about her closing statement. It had the sound of a threat, but the tone of a line of devotion. He thought to himself, School said a woman's actions could be too complicated to try and figure out…Oh well, I got to execute these plans that are dancing in my head. Crystal will no doubt run into a professional man that will marry her, take good care of her, and give her children…But I don't like that thought though. I shouldn't be so selfish and really shouldn't care, but I do.

When Friday night rolled around Dandy decided to go see Schoolboy and get briefed on happenings around town and always a wise word.

After listening to Dandy's encounter with Crystal School spoke, "Well son, your name is ringing and I hear you're doing good and taking giant steps. You told Crystal right, but reserve a spot for her if she ever does come back to you. Never slam an open door shut. When the chips are down you can depend on her because she has a big heart for you. So you want to travel…now you're looking down the line with vision. Most of the strolls are hot right now behind the tourist that got robbed and killed by a renegade hooker. Vice patrols will be relentless until they catch her, which won't be long, because the snitches are on high alert. Maybe you should pull up stakes and hit the road for a few months until things are back to normal."

Dandy agreed, "It's hot everywhere. Hollywood, Slauson, and Broadway, Western Ave, Sixty-Seventh and Central Avenue. Even Long Beach is dead. And Figueroa is smoking! Priscilla works out her book and won't like going to the out of town tracks, but she would rather face a firing squad than miss the trip and outwork the others. Also, I'm bailing one of my other ladies out every couple of weeks. Then the fixer is charging me dearly just to get thirty days or less for the ones with multiple offenses. I'm hitting the road before the weekend is over."

School agreed but warned, "Be careful, and you'll have to be armed. International fame comes with risks. Crossing state lines with intent to commit a crime is a federal beef. Other stuff can usually be paid off to the local rollers. Some of your game can get propped to cross you and get you a White Slavery charge. Your game could get kidnapped, or re-choose a lame from a town you land in. Just avoid the pitfalls and be cautious. Your homeboy "Murdock" is a ride or die henchman and will have your back.

It's a good idea to bring him along. And of course I'll be here for you if needed."

Murdock went to rehab and had been clean for six or seven months. They were friends since the sandbox days in grammar school.

Since Duchess was just into a six-month sentence he couldn't buy off, he put enough money on her books to hold her until they got back, or for her to join them if she got an early release.

***

The truck stop in Fresno was a pit stop for working girls from all across the country. Oakland had Market Street and San Pablo. And San Francisco had plenty money being spent on Divisadero St., Fillmore, North Beach, and the Tenderloin. Dandy hit and ran, never staying in one area too long. They hit Denver and worked The Five Point area, and the Red Light District in Salt Lake City, which is where Goldie left him and chose a pimp by the name of Sacramento Joe. School said the name of the game was cop and blow. But it balanced out because a sporting lady from Mid Town New York simply called "Red" came aboard ship and filled her boots with ease. Dandy flew home a few times a month to stash his money, then went right back on the road.

They hit Seattle, then Canada, and back to the states. Cherrie was killed in Montreal by an escaped mental patient. The ladies cried for days but slowly regrouped and fell in line like soldiers. Cherrie's family knew the life she chose but still had a hard time accepting her passing. They told Dandy that they had more than enough insurance to cover expenses but Dandy took care of all the arrangements anyway.

Within a week Dandy came up with fresh game. A veteran dame from Baltimore named Stormy. And a six-foot tall snow bunny named Laura. She was a plus size woman with huge blue eyes and an uncanny ability to excel when the rest of the crew slacked. She was a top flight pro. She also out paid Priscilla, Stormy, and Red, which really wasn't to Priscilla's liking at all. Murdock warned Dandy about the envy and jealousy that was brewing behind his back. But he shook it off and felt like it was good competition for the crew. It made them work harder to topple Laura.

Laura also posed as the manager of a girl's soul singing group and was able to rent rooms without drawing unwanted heat; they could move in and out of establishments discretely.

They left St. Paul and hit the south – Memphis, Atlanta, and Florida were profitable, but Dandy had to pay the local authorities on a few occasions. It was well worth it. Duchess had joined them in Atlanta and Dandy's bankroll began to swell. And so did the chaos. He thought about sending Priscilla and Duchess back home to work. Priscilla could manage things in his absence.

When he shared the thought with Priscilla she expressed her disapproval but ended it with assurance that if that was what he wanted, that was what she would do. She put shade on her insecurity and deep jealousy for Laura.

Dandy's name was internationally known and he had stacked enough money to start some of his dreams.

Dandy flew home in late Nineteen-Seventy-One to secure his bankroll and attend to other business. After dropping in on Schoolboy to chew the fat, and chop it up he flew right back to his game and an episode in his life he wished he could write off!

At the airport he was greeted by Federal Agents and a screaming Priscilla, "That's him! Dandy Dixon. He brought us here and forced us to sell our bodies." Duchess confirmed her testimony and Dandy knew he was a done duck.

Could it be a bad dream? Was this the end? Certainly it must be an illusion. But it was a cold vicious climax. He took a long deep look into Priscilla's bloodshot eyes with bad intentions in his.

He couldn't deny the charges. Maybe with just Priscilla's allegation, but with Duchess singing with her like two canaries he didn't have a chance. He had five years coming if he took them to trial and lost. He avoided trial and coped to the three and a half they offered. With a little good behavior he stood to be back on Broadway in a few years. He wondered what happened to his ladies, as long as he lived he would never forgive them, nor would he forget Priscilla and Duchess. The Feds tried to tie Murdock into the drama, but wound up releasing him to California to serve a short time violation of parole. Schoolboy always said things end the way they begin…but this definitely wasn't the end.

When School went to get Dandy's safe and other belongings the pad was empty. It was clean as Ole Joe's Turkey from the corner butcher. What clothes that were there had been ripped apart with a razor. Priscilla had left her calling card. Everything he acquired in life was gone. School had warned him years ago that it was a poor rat that only had one hole to stash stuff in. All he had was a penitentiary number to do and a heart full of vengeance and larceny for Priscilla.

Memories of Tracy rang a familiar bell as the sound of slamming gates vibrated in his ears. He drifted back to the last bit he did and the letters Crystal wrote for Priscilla. He tried to cast the thought of Priscilla and the years with her from his head, but the thought of breaking her kneecaps with a sledgehammer wouldn't leave. He wanted to slash her throat so that she could never tell another lie…or the truth for that matter. He knew it wasn't good to harbor such horrendous acts, but the demons wouldn't leave his mind.

55

Chapter 6

Mr. Poole

The ferry reached its destination, McNeil Island and Federal Penitentiary. The year was Nineteen-Seventy-Two. He was twenty-five and had one good thing on his side, and that was youth. He would still be in his twenties when he got released. At times he wondered if he would make it out alive. There were three stabbings in the first week he got there. But he knew his way around and how to avoid crucial situations. All his time was devoted to reading and exercise. Schoolboy couldn't write but he sent money regularly. His sister-in-law Freda occasionally wrote and kept him up on the boys and her and Ty's new family member, Fatima.

After nine months School sent word that Priscilla had been located. He had put a reward out for her whereabouts and it paid off. Dandy knew this day would come. He had friends throughout the country that knew what had gone down. No one would touch her. She was taboo. After cleaning Dandy out in California she dropped Duchess off in St. Louis and travelled around splurging like a celebrity.

Priscilla crossed Dandy out of jealousy and fear of loosing her status to Laura. Duchess went along with it because Priscilla had that much control and influence over her. Eventually Priscilla's conscious whipped her so bad she began using smack to try to erase the guilt and the fear of retaliation. When the money ran out she started turning tricks for drug money. She was hooked like a rabid dog. She was living in a sleazy motel on Imperial Highway in Watts, not far from the front, where she had easy access to the heroin that she had to have in order to function. Dandy instructed School and Murdock not to let anyone know of her whereabouts and not to harm her, just keep tabs on her. He wanted to deal with her personally.

After a year and a half of good behavior Dandy was transferred to Terminal Island, a lower custody institution, located in San Pedro near Los Angeles. There he ran into a few old friends like "Society Red", a hardcore pimp that only had boosters that went across country lifting furs, minks, and diamonds. He and his crew had gotten caught up crossing state lines with stolen merchandise. His homeboy Beaver was there from the Village. He got caught up filing for government grant money in numerous names. And a pimp from the Players Paradise Club named Black Diamond. He had flipped all his women out to the con, or the drag as he called it. He had a luxury mobile home and they played all across the country for years until a mark said he had gotten robbed because he was too ashamed to admit that he was swindled and gave the money freely without a threat. Just like McNeil Island, the joints were full of bank robbers, underworld bosses and soldiers, top-flight con men, polished hustlers and embezzlers - Black, White, Hispanic, Oriental, Indian and others.

Everyday Dandy walked the track taking in the fresh air off the ocean. He met an older dude that walked the track everyday as well. After several months they talked and became friends. One thing Dandy learned early from his first bit in prison was not to inquire too much about what a person was doing time for and how they got busted. They could have an appeal of conviction filed and don't want to discuss their case. You learn fast to mind your own business. In time you will know what a person is in for anyway. There are no secrets in prison. They are concentration camps with big ears.

He was out of Chicago and began as a Blackstone Ranger to the P Stone Nation and El Rukin influence. In the sixties he gravitated towards militant ideology, but after the dismantling of the Panther movement he slid into the mainstream 'fast life'. His forte was the con game and he was very proficient at it. His name was Lefty Upchurch.

After several months of conversation Lefty took Dandy under his wing and gave him all phases of the short and long con. From the ponzi schemes and variations of the pigeon drop and the donation to the three card monte. He also possessed a unique outlook on life and living with no hatred in his heart, as Dandy would soon learn.

One Saturday they sat in the bleachers of the baseball diamond while "Dino" and his team had batting practice for a game amongst convicts.

Lefty advised, "Watch out for the seagulls craping on you Dee."

"Yeah, they get on my last nerve!" Dandy screamed.

"Don't let them rattle you, they just doing what their instinctive nature has them to do. Same thing applies to that broad who had you placed here. The snake in her nature came out." Lefty admonished.

"Yeah Lefty, I made the mistake but she has to pay." Dandy assured.

"Now there you go. I told you that one has to be larceny free while executing con. The victims are the ones with the larceny. They think you're the sucker for being so nice, or think they are beating you out of something. You can't catch a vic if they don't have some degree of greed. Same thing applies to everything in life. The broad Priscilla will get hers. What goes around comes around and every dog has its day nephew. Worry can kill a person, and if you keep dwelling on her it can backfire on you. Chalk it up as experience. You bear some of the blame because nothing can happen to you if you're not in a position for it to happen. But if you allow yourself to be in a position to get played, crossed, beat, or whatever can and will happen. Position is key." Lefty schooled.

"But I was a Mack Man Lefty, I talked for it. I never hit a woman, put bruises on them or controlled them with force. If they wanted to leave I held the door open. That's what pains me, she lied and made me look like a gorilla pimp instead of the sweet Mack that I was."

"That's why I'm lacing your boots Neph. Let's see how well you talk for the big money. They went on with "class" until count time. Practice… Practice…Practice.

After count time Dandy paid a visit to another older convict that he had come to befriend and have conversations with. He talked to his homeboys from school days, Pot Tea, Crook, Pumpkin and Bean to stay abreast of news from the Village, and dudes from the street life that he knew before hand. But the O.G.'s enlightened and amused him with their war stories. They had game and Dandy stayed thirsty for knowledge.

Mr. Poole was one of them, along with Lefty. Mr. Poole changed his name to Abdul and was quick to explain that it meant Servant of God. He was a slender built man in his mid-fifties, bald headed with a full beard. He flashed an award-winning smile when Dandy entered his cell. "A Salaam Alaikum lil brother." He announced with glee.

"Good evening Abdul. How are you doing? I heard you went to the hospital today." Dandy said.

"I'm kicking, not high…but I'm kicking. And standing for the count by Allah's mercy. What be on your mind Dandy?" Mr. Poole asked.

"Nothing major, just checking on you before they rack the gates and cut the lights out." Dandy stated and added, "I was also wondering if getting visits made your time easier or harder?"

"A visit. What's that? Ain't had one in seven years I been down. I was told a long time ago that every tub stands on it's own bottom and I never forget the saying. Keeps me independent. My wife manages to send me a lil something every month, not much but something. They on the East Coast and I been in all West Coast pens. And I would never put that burden on my family. Plus I'm down to the wire now with just a year or so left" He whispered.

"I haven't received one either, I just needed to hear one of your life experiences before lights out." Dandy explained.

Mr. Poole smiled and said, "Speaking about hearing reminds me of the day I got busted for this bank robbery I'm doing ten on. Now you ain't Muslim Dandy but you was born one and that's another story for another night cause it's deep and will take time to explain. Anyway, no mater where I am, in here or out on the streets I have been taught to pray five times a day amongst other things. Before performing the prayer there is a call made to assemble and pray in congregation or in private. You follow me?"

"I'm with you sir." Dandy assured.

He continued, "Okay, so one morning my wife is crying and pressing me about bills and what we don't have and what we need. So I declare a time out to rest my ears and leave out the flat we had in Philly. I bring a handwritten note and aim for the first bank I saw. On the way I hear this call to prayer coming from a gym in the park I was walking across. I see shoes lined up outside the gym so I know they inside getting lined up to pray. What I was supposed to do was take my shoes off, bust on in the gym, wash up, and fall in line to pray. But the devil was whispering in my ear and telling me I need to go and get the money, but what I got was this time. That's the story about hearing and obeying. And as far as me going to the hospital today, they call me in to talk to the shrink every six or seven months. I used to go more often when I first got busted. When I went thru the physical the psych

60

asked me if I had a history of mental issues like seeing shit or hearing stuff. I told him I hear voices but it wasn't odd or abnormal to me. His eyes popped wide open and he asks how often I hear these voices. I tell this fool I hear them five times a day. By now he's ready to lie on the couch and let me ask him questions. He asked me what the voices said. It's the call to prayer I told you about. But I don't tell him that."

"Why not Abdul?" Dandy quizzed.

"Cause they already know I'm Muslim and if I told him it was a command to pray these idiots might think I might hear a command to blow something up. They would label me a terrorist and I might not ever get out this hell hole." He stated laughing. "Now hop in your cell before the gates rack," he warned.

"Thanks ole soldier, I needed to hear that. I'll see you in the morning."

"In Sha Allah, meaning God willing," was all that he said.

The following day he and Lefty went over their lines.

Dandy smiled and said, "You really remind me of Schoolboy. I swear you do."

"Never met Ole Schoolboy, but his reputation precedes him. He's well known and respected in the life. It would be a pleasure to rap with him one day."

Prison was depressing, but you do it a day at a time. It's a microcosm of the hood with reminders when to go to sleep, when to get up, when to go eat, and sometimes when to shower. The daily regiment get's old, but knowing you have a date for release is motivation to keep lying down and getting up.

Most convicts look forward to visits, some find them too depressing when it's over and you have to march back into prison life. Dandy delighted in visits, but he hadn't had one since his arrest so he was bewildered when his name was called over the loudspeaker one Sunday morning. Might it be Tyrone and Freda, perhaps one of his old girls had located him. Maybe Laura heard I was raising in six months and trying to get back on board? She would be perfect for the drag.

The suspense was cracked wide open like a breakfast egg when Crystal poured her smile all over him. Like fine wine she had begun to mellow with time. The baby face was more gracious, more motherly. A lovely preview of a mature woman.

Dandy stretched forth both hands. Took hers and held them dearly. She gazed at him but said nothing. He squeezed them lightly as he pulled her closer to him and kissed her just above the mole by her lips. He quickly flung his head back and said, "Hello stranger, I won't ask how you're been because I can clearly see you're still fine."

She blushed just like she did when he and Stanley first asked her and Priscilla for a date.

"How do you always manage to find me? Do you have a bloodhound in your possession?" He jokingly asked.

"There are a million Joe Browns and John Smiths in the world but only one Dandy Dixon that I easily found. I would have written but didn't want you to fall for another ghostwriter." She said.

They both smiled and Dandy lied, "I had forgotten the last one until you brought her up."

Crystal went on, "I came to tell you that I have been dating a man for about a year now and he has proposed to me. He's a doctor and really treats me well."

"Do you care for him as much as he cares for you?" Dandy inquired.

"I know I sound like a fool, but I care more for you than I do for him. I don't want to be in a committed relationship while having feelings for someone else. I told you I would wait for you and it still applies." She asserted.

"At this point I have nothing to offer than myself. Sounds like he has a foundation that is fortified with security and that's probably best for you." He said candidly.

"It is best for me but it's coming from the wrong person Dandy. I'm just the type of person who knows what I want, and who I want. If we can be together, I will cancel wedding plans with him and dedicate my life to us as I have told you before." She swore.

"Together on my terms or yours?" He quizzed.

"What's wrong with a compromise." She bargained

"Sounds just like me when I offered to cancel my relationship with Priscilla." Dandy fired back, "When a man wanders thru seeking solutions there is nothing wrong with a meeting of the minds if that meeting becomes the missing piece of the puzzle. But I know who I am and where I'm going. I'm stable and have purpose, values and goals in life. Now that I have explained myself the question is are you willing to grow with me under my guidance, direction, and protection?"

Crystal's face became stern as she spoke, "You have been talking or macking to those ladies you had way too long. You don't address me with that pimp talk Mr. Dixon, I'm not one of them."

"I know you are not cut from the same clothe as them and I apologize if my vocabulary rubs you the wrong way. That's just me, but I won't alter my ideology for you or no one else." He politely stated.

Crystal thought for a moment then said, "Dandy, I understand you and realize a man has to do what he feels he has to do."

"Good then, at least I know we don't have a failure of communication." He answered.

Crystal spoke to the point, "Will you at least try to get a job if we get together?"

"I hope not," He said with a smile. "The bottom line is you take me as I am, I know you want me to change. You wouldn't keep coming back repeatedly if you didn't see or feel something in me that makes your persistence worthy, and I might just change but it will be at the time of my choice, not your demand. And I mean that!"

Crystal sealed the conversation with, "Okay Dandy, I won't seek you out ever again. I pray you find happiness in your world, and I pray I find happiness in my fiancé."

The room became ice cold as they bid farewells.

Again Dandy felt the love pangs in his heart. It was challenging, but he shook it off and remained strong, firm, and rooted in his inner self.

***

Dandy focused his mind back to prison and dealing with the conditions of confinement. He had done most of the time and the time did not do him. He wanted Crystal, but he had a large ego and an ardent desire to keep his principles intact. He was released in the spring of Nineteen Seventy-Five. Not bad considering it could have been worse, but bad enough to vow he would never return. He was pushing thirty and had seen too many old grey men with a boatload of years left to do.

Lefty was getting out in another six months and then their plans could take root. Dandy had kept consistent conversation with a convict who was a real estate tycoon on the streets. His name was Mr. Goldstein. He gave advice on investing money to prisoners, and staff as well. He had also given Dandy a list of influential people to contact when his bankroll was right. That's where Lefty's plans came in – get a bankroll on the smooth side. He figured talking and faking for it was a minimal risk hustle. He was still a little gun shy about pimping. It would be nice to knock a dame and teach her the drag but that involved a lot of screening, time and most important, trust, which he was very thin on. If he and Lefty could knock a couple mega stings off as planned it would be all he needed to start some legal investments.

Dandy stayed with his brother upon release and his intensions were to just lay low until he and Lefty hooked up. On the third day home he'd just returned from Schoolboy's when a spanking, brand new money-green Nineteen-Seventy-Five Cadillac Fleetwood Brougham pulled in front of the house. A short, well-tailored man with a Super Fly hairdo jumped out and screamed in a high-pitched tone, "Come on out here Dandy Dee! This your ole partner Baby Talk.

Dandy greeted Baby Talk with delight. "What's happening Slick? You shinning like new money. How much that wood set you back for?"

"They was going for around three grand when you left, they above five now but when you got it you just drop the loot on the table and demand the keys."

"So what you doing Talk? 'Pimp or die' used to be your motto. Looks like the "P" been good to you." Dandy acknowledged.

"I'm on some advanced shit. Turned my game up a notch or two Dandy. I don't have streetwalkers no more. Pimping with the pen now. The credit card and forgery game is what my dames do." Talk explained.

Dandy peeped into the back seat and saw an extra huge woman; she had to weigh a good two hundred plus pounds. "Big Momma on your line?" Dandy quizzed while motioning toward her.

"Absolutely! That's Big Annie and she pay like she weigh. She got the gift of gab and don't miss when she goes to work. I got three more women at my condo. Big Annie has her own apartment. They all play like pro's and dig this Dandy, I don't ever want another dollar from a hooker unless she converts to the paper game." Talk explained matter-of-factly.

"I can dig it. You got to lace me up with that game one day." Dandy stated.

"You know it ain't no thang. You got that coming." Talk assured while peeling five C-notes for Dandy off a wad of money as fat as one of Tommy Hearn's' boxing gloves and added. "You're the guest of honor tonight at the club. All the regulars, and a few players from out of town are giving you a welcome home tribute."

"Thanks for the gaps to fill the empty lining of my pockets. But man, I don't know if I can make it Talk."

"You're welcome. You know how we do it when we got it. You like a brother to me. You got boss respect from everyone cause you always have remained the same. Ain't no big me…little you in your game. No sir. And one more thing, no bet to me player. Everyone is expecting you. And I delegated myself to bring you. I'll pick you up at ten." Talk demanded.

With not much of a choice Dandy spoke, "See you at ten. Besides, I need to see how this machine of yours rides."

The club was filled to capacity. Mack's had their bottom line ladies representing and co-signing any lie they told. Everyone was dressed to kill. Fast, Honey Cone, Blue and the Dripper. Slim, Big Ball, Sugar Lump, and good pimping B.H., and Chin were just a few faces Dandy immediately recognized in the crowd.

Plenty splurge and sport jumped off this night in his honor. They even had Mr. Holmes, the tailor, on deck to take Dandy's measurements for two tailor-made walking suits. The boosters had alligators to match, and everyone put some denomination of paper in a big pot. Big or small, it didn't matter. They did it like real players when times were good.

Diamond Shorty directed one of his ten women to take care of Dandy until told otherwise. "Don't worry Dandy, the rent for her flat is paid for a year and she can't say you turned her out. Not that she would, she's been tried and tested. She's a vet. She ain't no spring chicken but she knows how to treat a man." He assured. "She gonna pay you until you cop a dame to pay you."

The layout was just what Dandy needed and Cindy was a thoroughbred that treated him like he was her man. But she was his friend's woman and Dandy kept reminders that this was temporary. He stayed with Cindy for two weeks because he didn't want to misuse a kind gesture that very few, if any, would do. When hard luck hit Shorty a few years back Dandy gave him a bank to get back on his feet. Shorty tried to repay him back, but Dandy refused and told him not to steal his blessings. This was Shorty's golden opportunity to return the favor.

With gratitude and graciousness to Shorty, Dandy went back to his brother's, but not for long. He was riding with Baby Talk one evening when Talk parked near the stroll and went into the liquor store to grab some cigarettes. Dandy was waiting in the car when a red-head, freckle faced light skinned lady with a doll face approached him and questioned, "Aren't you Dandy Dee?"

Dandy sized her up and down before answering, "That's right, why you asking?"

"I'm Lil Bit, and I have heard all about you for years but never had the pleasure of meeting you."

"You look like a working girl Lil Bit and I would say get in, let's ride and kick it but I don't interfere with a woman trying to make her money, or her man's money." Dandy voiced.

"I don't have a man right now." She declared.

"In that case handle your business and I'll come thru after midnight." Dandy asserted. "If I see you we can talk." He decided he would take a chance on Lil Bit.

She replied, "I'll be looking for you." And swayed her small but shapely hips on down the pavement.

He immediately inquired about who she was and where she came from. Turned out she was with a local gambler who took care of her until he was killed over a dice game a few months back. She was small but packed a huge heart and a lot of energy.

That evening they talked and Dandy told her about the last lady he had that fell by the wayside and betrayed him. After she gave him the money she had made he spelled it out perfectly clear that he only needed a lady until the time came for him to leave town on other business and that would be the end of their relationship.

She agreed and said, "I need someone for various reasons; it doesn't have to be permanent. Will you put me on a plane for home when you decide to go because after you I don't think there will be another man in my life."

Dandy agreed, "We have a contract."

Chapter 7

The Sting

The woman stood parallel with the living room wall of a shabby smoke-stained room. She cut loose a hard sigh of relief at the sight of red swirling up the glass syringe. She untied the old nylon stocking that was tied around her arm very slowly with her teeth while mucus slid down her nose. She sniffled it back up as water from her eyes rolled down her cheeks. She bent over and as precise as a brain surgeon she squeezed the rubber bulb of the outfit, slowly and surely injecting the brown fluid.

Immediately her eyes began to dry and the tears ceased to flow. Her mouth was wide open like a corral gate and her eyes rolled back into her head. Like molasses she began to slide down the wall, and from a squatting position she bounced back up perpendicular to the wall. She repeated this regiment several times. She was in another world and unconscious of her actions.

Sleepy, the houseman of the shooting gallery barked, "Priscilla, I told your greedy ass to do half of that stuff first, you trying to kill yourself?"

"Ohh kayy baybee." She slowly dragged out her mouth while viciously rubbing her nose. "I'm trying to feel this shit." She slurred.

Sleepy was shocked and angered, "You should see how you look, you wouldn't feel strychnine bitch!"

"Don't be calling me a bitch Sleepy! I'm going to my pad." Offended, she stormed out the door and down the hall to her room.

Big head Benny, the doorman, hurriedly locked the door behind her as Priscilla strolled down the hall like the classy lady she once was. Closer observation revealed the face of too many sleepless nights and tobacco stains that ruined a once sparkling set of teeth. She had lost control of her hygiene and her total self. She had long since blown every dime of the money and assets she ran off with. Now she fed her habit by selling herself to anyone whose sexual needs were strong enough to bear her appearance.

As she opened the door of her unkempt room and stepped inside a strong force slammed it shut. She turned in terror and tried to scream at the face of Dandy. She sucked in air but couldn't release it. The entire heroin in her system was depleted and she stood as rigid as a plank of pine. Her eyes appeared to pop out of their sockets and her knees knocked uncontrollably. She gagged in an effort to release her air but darkness overtook her.

Dandy bent down over her crashed frame and snatched a glove off one hand and roughly shoved it under her left breast, only to see if she had just fainted. He reached for the syringe full of battery acid that Cotton, the dope-fiend concocted for him but his intentions were altered as he looked into a face that had experienced a vicious transformation.

He went to the roach infested sink and filled a burnt pot with water and threw it in her face. She immediately came to her senses and flinched in an effort to get up.

Dandy demanded, "Just lay there snake, don't get up."

"Dandy, oh daddy, please don't kill me!" Priscilla cried and pleaded.

He cut her off, "Shut up, don't even fix your lying mouth to speak. Just look at you tramp. You traded the life we had for this," as he surveyed the rumpled room. He pointed the syringe of tragic magic in her face and stated, "This is instant death and it's personally for you. But I don't think you deserve such relief, I can see you have been decaying for some time. You're not worth the risk of me walking the big yard for life. I still want to kill you, but you're already dead."

He threw the syringe on the floor and crushed it with his shoe, her panting slowed but her bulging eyes followed his every movement as he paced the floor.

"On second thought I hope you live a hundred more years, because misery and sorrow will be your dearest friends. You're trifling, you have no morals or values in you." With that he bent down and spit in her face then walked to the door, he put his gloved hand on the knob to exit but her voice stopped him.

"Dandy please allow me to explain."

He never turned around to face her as he spoke to the door, "I told you to be silent. Don't ever in life let my name roll off your lying tongue."

She cried herself into cramps and after several days of fear, guilt and lack of a will to live, Priscilla Parker's bloated body was found in her apartment. An apparent self -inflicted overdose put an end to her misery. She clutched a note in her hand that simply stated, 'I love you D.D.'.

***

71

Word of her suicide was chilling to hear, but didn't phase Dandy. He couldn't recall any good memories with her, because they were devoured by the bad ones. When he left her room he left all memories of her existence behind him.

Dandy's money was stacking. Lil Bit was quite sufficient and very impressive. He didn't attempt to recruit a stable because he only needed front money for the sting he and Lefty had plans for. He rarely went out except to visit Schoolboy or Tyrone.

One pre-dawn morning Lil Bit came in and placed her earrings on the dresser. The massage parlor she worked out of was a good front and the clientele was choice white-collar executives.

Dandy smiled at his little four foot eleven woman with a heart as big as all outdoors and said, "What's happening lil Momma?"

"You and me." Was her slick reply.

Dandy was propped up on the bed in a rich green silk smoking jacket reading when she came in, but now he found himself watching this pretty, petite woman as she took her boots and clothes off and went to bathe. He was going over how he was going to tell her that he was leaving. He couldn't tell her he was going to Chicago, nor could he mention Lefty's name.

Feeling fresh and relaxed she put a robe on and asked, "Can I get you anything?"

Dandy answered, "No love, just come here." Bluntly he added, "I have to be in Canada on Monday, that is the day I told you about when you first got with me."

With tears forming in her eyes she begged, "Baby, I know we had an agreement and I respect you laying out the conditions before I got caught up with you, but I guess I allowed my emotions to get the best of me. I really couldn't help myself. I never told you, but I never knew anyone like you existed. I feel possessed, yet so free with you." She mixed a smile with tears continuing, "You don't say much, but I love your strange, or better said, different style and want to stay with you, can I come with you? I'm in too deep to quit."

"No you can't, you would be in the way. I told you all this on day one." Dandy affirmed.

"Well can I stay here? I don't want to go home." She pleaded.

"You can stay, but I'm done. I can't guarantee I will even come back." He stated matter-of-factly.

"I'll keep the apartment and manage. If you come home I'll have your money waiting for you." She declared with confidence.

Dandy nodded his head and said, "We shall see and if I do come back, I'll bring you a souvenir."

With that they embraced and for the second time since they had been together, they made love. Intense love that put them into a deep sleep.

***

Dandy's flight touched down in O'Hare Field five minutes after the estimated time of arrival. A slim and very beautiful female security guard noted the sleek young man with a perm hairdo, dressed in a silver grey three-piece Petrocelli suit with a burgundy shirt, burgundy tie, burgundy shoes by Gucci, and a white full length camel hair top coat with a burgundy and grey checkered wrap. As he strolled thru the airport with roller luggage, she was captivated. The charismatic movement of Dandy entranced her. When he stopped at a gallery of phone booths she snapped and thought, What's come over me, I see thousands of handsome men come thru here everyday. And then she continued her rounds.

The ever so dapper Dandy dropped a coin in the phone and dialed a number from his notes. A charming voice spoke from the other end, "Hello, may I help you?"

Dandy cleared his throat and said, "Yes, this is Dandy Dee is Lefty in?"

"No but where are you, I'm supposed to pick you up."

"I'll be at the bar in the main lobby of O'Hare." He stated.

"Be there in thirty minutes." She agreed. Without a goodbye they hung up simultaneously.

Dandy ordered a virgin daiquiri. He had been staring thru the glass windows onto the runway where planes trafficked to and from all corners of the world. A familiar voice startled him but he never showed it as he turned around and made eye contact with a dark ebony goddess in her late thirties. She was garbed in a milk white jumpsuit and white boots. She had a business like mask on as she asked, "Mr. Dixon?"

"Yes, Dandy Dee here."

She never changed expressions as she began to speak; obviously she was very well disciplined. "Hi, I'm Tonya, Lefty's woman, are you ready?"

Dandy grabbed his luggage and stated, "Never more so. I've heard a lot about you."

"Good things, I'm sure."

"Absolutely." Dandy assured.

Lefty's crib was located in Evanston, a small suburb just outside of Chicago. It was plush. Lefty's skill at con paid off and it showed. He was a boss player in the game. His one mistake was living too flamboyant without a stated income. That's what sent him to federal prison. He was very adamant about paying taxes. He always said the government was like the mafia. They want their cut of any money you make. He was fortunate to have a woman like Tonya; she managed to salvage the few things he had left while he was gone. Dandy tipped his hat to her, as his luck with women wasn't nearly as good.

"Can I get you a refreshment while you wait." She asked.

"Do you have a ginger ale?" he requested.

She smiled for the first time and said, "Sure," as she went to a small icebox that was located behind the bar. After serving him she added, "You can play some music if you like," pointing to a stack of several albums. "I'm going upstairs, if you need anything just holler. Lefty said he would be here within the hour."

Dandy found an Eric Dolphy album entitled "Last Date" He put it on and kicked back in meditation. Before it ended Lefty came thru the door clad in an Edwardian cut pin striped three-piece suit with topcoat and hat. Dandy rose to his feet and shook his friend's hand, "Say old man, you about as sharp as a Philadelphia lawyer! How you feeling this freedom?"

Lefty laughed and stated, "We mix real well, I can dig this kinda thing from now on. And what you mean 'old man' chump, I can still pass for forty." With that they broke into laughter.

Tonya came down to rest Lefty's coat and hat. After she poured him a drink. Lefty asked Dandy, "Do you want a stick of this Chi Green gangsta weed?" Before Dandy could say pass it to me, Lefty continued "Better enjoy it now, we start work tomorrow and have to keep clear heads. Won't be none of this." Lefty reached into his vest pocket and pulled out a gold snuffbox full of cocaine. "Or this either."

Dandy assured, "I don't indulge in hard drink or drugs anyway, and I'm not excessive with the weed. I don't over indulge in anything accept money."

Lefty commented, "And remember that money is just a vehicle to take us to our needs and desires. It can also take one to his or her destruction. Total obliteration. Life is a test nephew. But now we need to focus on our mission, let's get this money first. How have you been doing with your Spanish?"

"Me va bien," Dandy said.

"Very good. Because you won't be saying much but what little you do we will be communicating in Spanish. I have a scar to put on the side of your face and some other props I got from a partner who is a make-up artist for the movie studios. I've been practicing using my right hand. It's hard but practice makes perfect and we have wigs, temporary teeth and other disguises. Because she will definitely put a reward and contract out for the two elderly South Americans who played her out of her money."

Dandy was all ears as Lefty continued, "The stage will be the city they named twice because it's so nice. And twice as hard to survive in, but if you survive it you can survive anywhere in the world. It's New York Jose, I keep calling you that because I'm disciplining myself. I don't want to make an error. A slip of the tongue has caused many ships to sink. But back to our sting, we will rehearse our lines in the morning. We have to act as well as W.C. Fields when the curtain came up in Harlem. The victim of the illusion

76

is Miss Fontella Brown, the numbers queen. I've been studying her for a long time. The price of admission is a cool million, half a million apiece. I know for a fact that she's worth ten times that much in cash alone and that ain't counting other assets, but she might back off if the stakes are too high."

Dandy continued to sop up all the game Lefty put out. "Nothing is guaranteed when you're playing but we can stack most of the odds in our favor. The main thing, the only thing, we have is the fact that she is greedy and is always looking for something for nothing. She is fat, wealthy and very street wise, but like I taught you, this game is called con, short for confidence. If we are successful at gaining her confidence she will be ready for plucking. She has no ties to organized crime, she has a small cadre of flunkies and two bodyguards she pays well but they ain't no worry. They won't see anything coming just like she won't. I would give half my share to see the look on her face when the veil is lifted. She's in her late fifties and not a bad looking mark, but money can do wonders. Not only does she run numbers, she fences anything from steaks to rare stamps. A good hustler, but as I told you, all is fair in love, war, and the con. Some players say they won't play certain people but they lying. They will tell a lie to anyone and their self. If a vic bites they gonna reel the hook on in. Bar none! But I am selective with marks that I put an eye on. I won't play certain people, guess that's why my luck with this game has been good."

After dinner and a good night's rest they got up just before dawn and prepared to leave separately. Lefty spoke, "We will check into separate hotels. Go over the script backwards and forward. I need this last lick to buy that ranch I told you about. Me and my woman are going to raise chinchillas and live in grand fashion ever after. God willing."

Dandy affirmed, "I have plans too if all turns out well and I feel it will. We might get Academy Awards for this one."

Lefty had been unsuccessful in getting close to Miss Brown but the word was out that he wanted to do some form of business. He patiently waited for her to respond.

Dandy was kicked back on the king sized bed when he decided to order room service. He picked up the phone and said, "Servicio de habitaciones, por favor." He ordered dinner in Spanish with a few flaws but got the message across. After eating he had the switchboard operator dial Lefty's room.

"Hello, these be Mr. Lopez, can I help you? Lefty said in broken English.

Dandy answered with a Latin accent, "Miguel my friend, how are you?"

In preplanned dialogue Lefty said, "Jose! Ahh, long time no talk to you my friend."

"Has Miguel made talk with the real estate agent yet? I no like it these crowded condiciones of the big city." Dandy said in Spanish.

Lefty grimaced and declared, "Be of patient mi compadre, you no worry. She will call."

About an hour later Lefty was invited, by messenger to a party for Miss Brown. The messenger stated that she would talk to him when he arrived.

Lefty thought out loud as he showered and got dressed, Dam! They say the darkest hour is just before dawn. Dandy was getting impatient and frankly so was I. Lefty sealed the mangy-grey hairpiece and mustache in place and slipped into the elevator shoes he and Dandy had to increase their height. He looked in the mirror and said to himself, "Miss Brown! Ahh, it be the great pleasure of Miguel to finally meet you." He grabbed a cane and walked to the door with gimpy steps.

The old Cotton Club on 125th St. was newly renovated and packed to capacity. Champagne flowed as mostly people of the nightlife gathered in small groups making big chitchat. The dance floor was full as it's inhabitants stepped and slid to a ten-piece rhythm and blues band. It looked more like a fashion show as people from all walks of life were lit up for the festivities. Lefty felt out dressed and certainly out of place, but quickly remembered that his plain attire was exactly how he was supposed to look. He didn't want anything to say slick or hip. Tables were lined around a twelve-foot long bar top that held a ten-foot long sheet of triple deck birthday cake.

After nearly a half hour of observation Lefty made his presence known to a goon wearing a dark suit and shades. He was posted in one place all the while Lefty was there so he knew he was on post. The goon left and returned a few minutes and escorted him to a room backstage.

Moments later, an overly healthy woman in a money green double knit St. John suit with matching handbag and a wide brimmed Fedora held the floor. She had a silver fox mink comfortably draped across her shoulders and the attention of five or six guests as she talked with wide mouth and plump hands that displayed diamond clustered rings on every finger. After ending her speech she spied Lefty thru diamond studded eyeglasses and spoke, "Mr. Lopez I presume, are you comfortable? Can I have anything brought to you?"

"Yes, very comfortable. And it be the pleasure of Miguel to extend to you the happy birthday wish." Lefty obliged.

She smiled but strained to process the dialogue of her distinguished guest. She wasn't sure if the light brown-skinned man was Puerto Rican, Cuban, or Columbian. She didn't want to expose any lack of knowledge, so she didn't ask. After introducing her friends she asked them to excuse herself and Lefty. A bodyguard hesitated and cut his eyes back and forth from Lefty to his employer. She caught his actions and silently beckoned for him to leave.

She began, " Have a seat Mr. Lopez." He leaned back in the leather chair next to him as she added, " You are very persistent Sir. My colleagues have informed me that you have refused to deal with them."

Lefty studied the stout woman with a mouth full of gold teeth. She was very cultured and obviously wealthy. And the power she was accustomed to was very apparent.

After lighting a Garcia Vega Lefty spoke, " Yes, this be what you call it ahh, correcto."

She cut a slight smile at his accent and was obviously intrigued at his indifference.

With a stern face he explained, I be want to talk about the huge green ones, my cousin in Spanish Harlem say you be the one who buy anything of value regardless of cost and I no waste my time with the small fry. Miguel no talk to the leetle people." He frowned as though the thought of small timers put a bad taste in his mouth and continued, "I come to the big city to make the big deal but my people no show."

More confused than anything else, she asked, "Mr. Lopez, what are you talking about?"

Lefty smiled and capped, "Miguel speak about the green back dollar. It be not real. But it have real look and real feel. It be number one!"

Her eyebrows arched upward while handing Lefty an ashtray. " I see, you have counterfeit. How good is it and at what price?" She inquired.

Lefty smiled as he took it with his right hand and said, "First you see, then we do the talk. But I be for the big deal, not the small one."

She assured with a stern face, "I have enough capital to invest in anything that creates a profit, but why me?"

Lefty was ready, "Maybe no you. I wait on me buyer for several days before I contact you. I allow him one more day, cause he never late before. He no show and Miguel have to sell pronto."

With doubt on her face she said, "Okay but I haven't seen or heard about any funny money in years, and I always know when things like that hit the streets."

Again Lefty was prepared, "Ahh, you no hear or see never. My contact take it across the big pond to Europe, or Asia. I not sure, but never here."

She nodded in agreement to something that was not crystal clear, but it was logical to her.

Lefty stood up, put one hand on his waist and with the other he pointed one finger in the air as if he was trying to see which way the wind was blowing and said, "I know what we do. You come to Miguel's room and I show you a sample."

"I don't do business outside first hand, but if I make an exception I will come with escorts." She demanded.

"No." Lefty barked and added, "If Miguel trust you, then you trust Miguel." He was only testing her. He knew she would never walk into a set up, a potential robbery. But he also knew that she was nipping on the bait very eagerly.

"It can be no other way. I'll look at the goods and if they are what you say they are we can make a deal. We meet at a designated location and transact business. I will have someone deliver the money immediately as we seal the deal." She instructed.

They agreed to meet at noon the next day in Lefty's room. Dandy would be thrilled to hear things were going as planned.

The following day at about twelve ten in the afternoon Miss Brown came to Lefty's room with two male companions. The bulge in their suit coats didn't surprise Lefty at all. He knew Miss Brown wasn't a hijacker, nor was she going to get hijacked.

Lefty greeted them, "Good afternoon Miss Brown please have a seat and excuse me for one moment. Me have a guest who was just leaving."

He left the room and entered the bathroom. In about three minutes he and Dandy emerged from the bathroom carrying two briefcases. "This is my associate, his name be Jose." Lefty said.

Dandy was decked out in a chocolate brown three-piece suit, beige shirt and tie; dark shades and a three-inch scare across his left cheek to camouflage his appearance. Capped off with a Panama hat that they purposely put on because no one from the East Coast would wear a straw hat in the winter like they would in South America.

They spoke in Spanish for a few seconds before the door knocked. It was the bellhop who carried the two suitcases for Dandy.

Hurriedly before they opened the door Dandy snapped one brief case open and peeled two hundred dollar bills off one of the Michigan stacks of money, gave it to Lefty and slammed it shut before rushing to the door to have the bellhop assist him.

Dumbfounded, Miss Brown looked at Lefty and asked what was going on.

"I be the sorry one but as I told you, the buyer had one more day to contact me and Jose. This bill is for you to examine."

Miss Brown took it with amazed eyes; the touch and look were flawless.

Lefty continued, "The buyer contact me early this morning and as you saw my compadre deliver to them now."

Looking totally defeated she asked, "When will you have more Mr. Lopez?"

Looking sad, Lefty hunched one shoulder up to his head and said, "Miguel not know, never know until I receive. Maybe tomorrow, maybe next week, maybe next month but soon I hope. My friend Jose and myself are from Peru, we be Afro Peruvians. The product we get is called the 'Peruvian Note,' it be the world's finest fake money in the world. We were told that a new dollar is soon to come out and the organization I work for is making the changes already before it come out. So maybe they give me more of what you have, or it will be a wait for the new dollars. Very sad you missed the good deal, but I contact you when I have more."

"Please do Mr. Lopez, I hope to hear from you soon." With that said she and her muscle departed.

Lefty smiled with a sense of accomplishment, he had Miss Brown exactly where he wanted her. He knew she would have someone go out of town to pass the bills. The real money surely would pass and only build her anticipation. Lefty didn't want to show any eagerness, so like a good pot of gumbo he let it simmer.

After another week Miss Brown called to see if there was any news. Purposely Lefty and Dandy let her continue to wait. A few days later Lefty arranged a meeting over lunch at a restaurant on Lennox Avenue.

Lefty, Dandy and the victim sat in the far booth while the bodyguards stood outside as they dined. That was a good sign of trust Lefty concluded.

Lefty opened the conversation of business at hand, "Miss Brown, we have what to be the final run of these bills. It be very big package, no more at least the one year period."

Dandy capped the line off in very broken English, "That be thee true talk. You need it the what you call umm."

Lefty immediately took over as planned, "Miss Brown, my partner wants to say he has an investor that can put money with your money if needed."

"Well just how much are we talking about?" She asked.

"We talk of the five million perfect one hundred dollar bills. You pay one million. Lefty proclaimed. She raised her hands to take off her glasses and nearly forgot she was in public, but caught herself and toned her reply down, "Five million!"

Lefty thought he threw too much at her when she declared, "If these are as good as what I saw then I want them all, and I don't have a need for a partner." Her ego had kicked in and so did her ability to negotiate. "Now do to the volume I am prepared to give you eight hundred thousand, not one million."

Lefty emerged and nearly stood up out of his seat with a frown and stated, "NO, I make it no horse trade. One price, no more, no less. I no bicker around, you take at the price I give or I go to the big Italian man that I know. I only give you, the charming and very beautiful one first opportunity."

She squirmed in her seat like a wiggle worm in heat because of the flattery, but still persisted, "I don't know about anyone else but I'm prepared to have all the money we agree on this evening. No exceptions and that should deserve some degree of deduction." Lefty listened to her proposal, "Let's say fifty thousand. I will give you nine hundred and fifty thousand."

Lefty knew a bird in the hand was worth more than ten in the bush but didn't want to jump too fast. After a moment of silence he spoke, "Very well, we have a deal."

Dandy nearly blew it with the wide grin he displayed. Lefty immediately kicked him under the table to grab his attention and stick to the script. Lefty shot Dandy a C-note and said in broken English, "Pay for the bill Jose." He faced Miss Brown and said, "Be right back I go to the men's room."

Dandy and Miss Brown proceeded to the counter, paid the tab, and left a tip.

When Lefty came out he had a worried look on his face and whispered to both of them, "Did the cashier give you the funny look?"

"No" Miss Brown said curiously. "Why do you ask?"

Lefty stated nervously, "I give to you thee wrong money to pay thee bill. I gave to you the fake money by accident."

"Well it passed without a hint of a problem, let's make preparations for the exchange."

They departed after instructions and Lefty said to himself, she's got that serious itch to get trimmed, I could let her orchestrate the drag from here on out.

The transaction was set to go down in the bus terminal that Dandy had already placed two large luggage cases in locker number 711. They were filled with stacks of play money with real hundred dollars on top of each one.

Miss Brown walked and Lefty limped thru the thick of the evening crowd listening to the arrivals and departures. They walked to be sure no one was following them. When they came to locker number 711 Lefty came out of his pocket with the key and opened the locker. He bent down and cracked open the suitcase and flashed its contents. He closed it and opened the other case and fanned through the bills with the original landing on top.

Miss Brown lurked over his shoulder and just when she began to speak Lefty slammed the locker shut and locked it, "It's all there Miss Brown." He assured the victim.

Her arrogance kicked in, "I've been counting money all my life. I'm a very successful woman and I know stacks of money when I see them. It's there or thereabouts. I can smell the amount."

They headed to the parking lot where Dandy and her henchmen awaited by her Rolls Royce. She ordered them to pop the trunk. Lefty opened the luggage and searched thru the bills. The only thing that beats a cross is a double cross and Lefty made sure he and Dandy didn't get played. Dandy grabbed the luggage and Lefty gave Miss Brown the key to the locker. The key he switched. He had a fake key made with #711 stamped on it as a little added insurance to stall them.

The goons went to retrieve the locker luggage full of heartaches, as Dandy and Lefty lit into a cab and sped off toward the highway. At the cross corners Lefty instructed the cabbie to turn into a mini mall and they excited to an awaiting car that Lefty's woman Tonya was driving. After loading the trunk with the suitcase and travel luggage, Lefty jumped into the passenger seat and Dandy flopped down in the rear. Lefty reached back with an open palm and Dandy gave him a high-five victory slap. The three of them laughed and relaxed.

"Hit the highway Tonya and keep an eye in the rear view, we driving home. It's going to take about twelve hours but we can alternate under the wheel. We have too much cargo to be boarding a plane." They tore off disguises and Dandy started thinking about future success. He also thought about Lil Bit, but things turned out just as he thought they would. They had invested over five grand but the dividends were well worth it.

"We hit a grand slam Dee, but the stadium was empty. No one must know about the lick we hit. We don't brag, we don't talk about it period. Let's make that vow right here and now." Lefty insisted.

They arrived safely about ten A.M. the next morning, chopped the money up and bid their farewells. And agreed not to contact one another for a couple of months.

Chapter 8

All That Glitters Ain't Gold

The ride up Century Boulevard was swift as the taxi cut thru traffic. Dandy noted that the Century stroll was more alive than before. Streetwalkers strolled and glanced over their shoulders, while bolder ones stood stationary and beckoned at prospective clients; they were camouflaged by the racetrack crowd, ticket holders of the event at the Forum Arena, and traffic slowing flowing to and from LAX. But to the trained eyes of Dandy Dee Dixon, the tricks, vice and rest of the underground figures were in plain view as they mingled in the urban setting. The cab continued across Century and hit the Harbor Freeway, exiting on Florence Ave then down to San Pedro, finally coping a left at an all too familiar corner where Cowboy busted him, and on to Schoolboy's.

He was inquisitive about all the details as usual. And Dandy knew School's lips were sealed. A pack of wild buffalos couldn't run a word out of his mouth. After Dandy ran the series of events down School pulled out a bottle of aged Remy and they had a toast. He refused the money Dandy tried to give him so Dandy secretly planned to buy him a gift of jewelry or clothing.

School cautioned Dandy not to return to the Apple for any reason whatsoever, disguise or no disguise. Also, not to flash and spend a lot of money in public. Dandy talked about getting a new Lexus or Benz, but School demanded he get a used one for now.

School tapped the night old ashes from his pipe and packed it with a fresh mixture of cherry blend tobacco. After three long drags he blew the cloud of smoke out and said, "Dandy my boy, you have done very well for yourself, despite the few stumbling blocks along the way, but you're back on track now. With the bankroll you have you don't need the hustle, not from the streets. You put your life into making money, now make the money work for you like rich folks do. Invest in something legal. Then if you just want to explore into an underworld venture your legit business will be your shade and keep you out the limelight. You see game is to be played and backed off of when you gain enough capital like buying precious metals, stocks, property, and things that will yield profit. With me, as with many others, the life has become just that, a way of life. I'm financially secure and could settle down on some farm and sit on the porch and smell jasmine all night. But I do what I do out of love and comfort. You love the fast life too and I'm not trying to square you up, I'm trying to wise you up. See I'm long in the tooth and too far-gone like being all in with a poker hand. Hell! I know drug dealers who been filthy rich for decades but they still dealing. Why? Because they hooked on the power that comes with it. They can have a dame, or a lame do what ever he tells them to do. You have youth on your side. You ain't thirty good yet. But time is a thief son, make up your mind now because you will look up very soon and wonder where it all went."

"I plan on investing in legal projects. I have to go see a good friend this week and talk. An old Jewish dude I met in prison." Dandy said.

"Just don't reveal how big a bank you have, always stay low key. Don't even let your left hand know what your right hand holds." School admonished.

School poured them another small shot of Remy and drank to peace and happiness. Then School declared, "I dam near forgot to tell you and I don't like being the bearer of bad news, but maybe it's good news."

"What is it?" Dandy wanted to know.

"I'll tell you because you going to hear it anyway and I know you man enough to deal with it but it's about Lil Bit."

Dandy sat with attentive ears, he was going to go to the spot he left her in when he left School's. But perhaps he wouldn't. And just maybe he wouldn't give her the silver fox waist length mink jacket he had planned to give her.

Schoolboy cleared his throat and the taste of cognac from his palate and spoke, "When you have something that's yours, let's say a woman. If you set her free and she returns she's yours to love. If she doesn't return she was never yours in the first place and you can't miss nothing you never had. Is that enough said?"

"You know I cop jive School" Dandy said with a smile and continued, "Right on School. You know you raised me old school. It seems like I be getting the sour end of relationships with women but like I been groomed, it's a blessing to get a dame out your mix now as opposed to later. Who she with?"

"Some young up-coming cat they call Slick. Ain't heard nothing bad about the guy's character but always keep your eyes open." School advised.

"For sure." Dandy replied.

Dandy went to he and his brother's pad to rest. That morning he sat with Tyrone and gave him a fat roll of hundred dollar bills and told him to put them up for him. Tyrone had taken a small loan out on the house and Dandy gave him the money to pay it off. He took all the kids and bought them a complete wardrobe to last two summers. Him and Tyrone went to the bank and opened up Certificates of Deposit for all of them. Ten thousand each would acquire a nice nest egg for college. Finally he gave Freda a few hundred to buy her self something pretty.

Dandy told Tyrone not to mention a word to anyone about his good fortune. He then went and bought a used black on black sport rag top Benz and shot to the pad he left Lil Bit in. He rode with the top down, the wind blowing in his face, and the radio blasting a jam by the Isley Brothers. Turning up Crescent Heights Boulevard, he thought about Lil Bit and her misfortune.

He had a key but knocked on the door out of respect and announced himself. The door cracked open and a young guy around twenty-one with a super-fly perm said, "Come on in Dandy."

Dandy addressed the thin dark-skinned man with no hair on his face as if he knew him, "What's happening Slick?"

"Just this pimping, you know." He answered proudly.

Dandy sat down without an invite and said, "I can dig it."

At that moment Lil Bit came into the living room with a cup in her hand. She had to come thru the living room to get to the kitchen. But it was more out of curiosity than a need to retrieve anything from the kitchen. At the sight of Dandy her face turned into that of a Benedict Arnold as she dropped her head in shame and spoke without looking up. "Hello and how was your trip?"

"Dandy and delightful." He smiled and asked, "How was yours?

She stuttered out, "…ahh…I have chosen Slick."

Dandy gazed at Slick and said, "Well player I wish you all the luck in the world. You'll need it. I just came for my few belongings. I knew all along your woman wouldn't hold up under pressure."

Slick snapped his fingers and told Lil Bit to bring all of Dandy's possessions. She scurried off like a trained pup.

"I hope there are no hard feelings. I know you know how it goes." Slick declared.

Dandy threw up both hands and announced, "Hey partner, I respect the game. I know if you're good to it, it will be good to you. I'm a gentleman and harbor no ill feelings towards you or her."

"I'm glad you don't and I got your dues she made for you up until the day I knocked her. I don't want it ever to be said that Slick was petty or small."

Dandy pushed back the stack of bills and said, "No Slick, you're a true player and whatever money the dame had when she chose you is yours." Dandy lied, "I need the ends and this is no reflection on you but I don't want, or need a weak broad or her money. She just made space for a real woman to take her place. You know it won't be long before I'm back on top of the world."

Slick grinned and said, "You're a bona fide player Dandy, and can't no one say anything ill about you in my presence without a squabble. I'm all about the understanding but I was pat for misunderstanding as well." As he reached back behind his waistline and put his hand on his rosco. He clasped his hands back together and continued, "I don't know how you would react to all this."

Dandy flashed a broad grin and touched a shoulder holster strapped under his coat and said, "Me and you both."

They roared together with laughter.

Lil Bit had been listening from the bedroom and came in the living room with a suitcase and a cardboard box. Slick helped him carry the possessions to Dandy's ride. Dandy thanked him and asked if it was okay with him to give his woman a souvenir from Canada that he promised her.

Slick answered, "Yeah Dandy it's okay cause you promised before I knew her."

Dandy grabbed the fox jacket and Slick gazed in amazement as they walked back to the apartment.

"Here's the present I promised, you know how I value my word. He slung it on the floor at her feet and spun around in a sweeping motion towards the door. He looked at Slick and said, "Pimp her hard."

Slick secretly admired Dandy's proficiency. While Lil Bit wished she could have told Dandy that she had expected a call while he was gone nearly a month, and when he didn't call she didn't think he was ever going to return. It mattered to her but not to Dandy. He chalked it up as another woman that bit the dust.

***

A money manager named Mr. Sherman who was a friend of Mr. Goldstein made Dandy's money work. In six months he had opened a booking agency and had several local entertainers under contract. He had money in the bank drawing interest and after another six months his high-

93

fashion men's clothing store with a barbershop, manicure, and facial lounge on top was bustling. Also, he purchased a two-unit rental flat. His joint on Melrose Avenue next to the Players Paradise Club was patronized by all the players and entertainers, local and out of towners as well.

Business was booming and Dandy was living the life from a different vantage point that he had never seen before. He had people managing his businesses and he simply collected money. He saved some, spent some, and always reinvested most of his profits for another year.

His home in Beverly Hills was a designers dream and only a few influential people knew where he laid his head every night. Schoolboy told him he was moving too fast and to slow down. But the glitter and glamour was hypnotic.

Women came at him from all angles but he never let any one of them earn the right to say he was their man. He was living the single life to the max. Life was sweet but he knew the day was coming where he would have a main woman, or even a wife to share what he considered to be the good life. Maybe they'd even have children. But it would take one hell of a woman to stand in the boots of the females he had relations with.

He thought about Crystal but surmised she was probably a mother of a little family by now with all the trimmings. He no longer considered himself a pimp and didn't want another sporting lady.

After checking on his business at his office he went to his health club and received a steam and rub down. Afterwards he entered the Players Paradise. He set the bar up and socialized with a few friends. Later that evening, he left for Nicks on Sunset to have a lobster dinner. A musician who did studio work noted him and spoke in a Cuban accent, "How are you Mr. Dixon?"

"Fine Mr. Castro and yourself?" He asked.

The short pudgy man with a beard replied, "Money is tight, but I'll make it. May I join you?"

Dandy pointed to the chair on the opposite side of the table and said, "It would be my pleasure."

After small talk about the music industry, Mr. Castro changed the subject, "Mr. Dixon, you are a scholar and a gentleman. I like you because you use your brains and help people in need. We go way back to the days when you didn't have as much success. Don't let one bad apple ruin your crop."

Dandy asked him to be more specific and he voiced, "There are a lot of people who would love to see you fail and become broke simply because of your color. They smile and do business but curse you under their breath. Also, and more importantly, you should take inventory of your employees. I won't call any names and I don't usually interfere with a man's business but I feel like you need to know about the activities of some of your employees. I seldom misjudge people and I could be wrong, but check it out for your safety and security. Thanks for the dinner Mr. Dixon." As fast as he appeared, he vanished.

Dandy racked his brain and immediately hired an investigator to peep into the lives of his employees. Two weeks later, he entered the office door of McFarland and Lee Private Investigators. A blond-headed man of middl age scanned over his notebook as Dandy sat at his office desk.

He cocked his elbow on the table that supported his forefinger that planted on the side of his face as he spoke, "Mr. Dixon we have conclud our research and learned that none of your people appear out of ordinary, however, we found one thing of interest. We couldn't get a na but someone in your booking agency deals cocaine from your offic suggest we install cameras to get proof of their identity. I don't know if are aware of this news or not, but I only work for you. Meaning what yo is your business, but if I found out these things then it won't be long before the authorities find out if they don't already know." He looked at Dandy for an expression.

Dandy sat expressionless for a moment, then spoke, "Here is the balance of the payment. And you're rehired. He peeled off a roll of hundred dollar bills and screamed, "Get that name!"

He spun around in the chair and headed to the door. He tossed the names around in his head to no avail. While driving he thought out loud, Someone's using me as a front and I don't like it. Won't have it! He didn't need the heat. He had once thought about dealing to a few choice people on the side but dismissed it because it wasn't worth the risk and things were going too well. Wow! Now I'm the sucker and fall guy. I have to nip this at the bud immediately. No, I have to up root it.

He headed home to clean up his pad. He always had an ounce or less around for close associate's social use.

The big box black Benz swooped up the driveway and before the engine had completely stopped Dandy was placing one foot out the door. He fumbled thru a ring of keys and after deactivating the house alarm he opened the service porch entrance. He never saw the two white men in suit and tie, but they made their presence known when he attempted to close the door behind him with a back arm stroke.

Thousand Eyes shoes intercepted his efforts and a voice spoke before he turned around. "Good afternoon Mr. Dixon."

Startled, Dandy spun around and made eye-to-eye contact with the barrels of two three fifty-sevens.

The voice spoke, "Federal Agents, you're under arrest!"

Dandy stood still and the next moments of silence seemed like hours.

His whole life flashed before him. This had to be the Coup de Grace. The thought of loosing sight on the world again and rotting away in a cell was a cold-blooded déjà vu.

The two men stood in front of him and the older spokesman ordered him to turn around and face the wall. The other young rookie nervously held his weapon on Dandy's frame. This was the rookies' first year on duty and his greenness was evident. They handcuffed Dandy and just as he was about to ask what was the meaning of all this, the rookies' gun discharged and Dandy's body was plastered on the wall by the impact of a piercing slug of lead.

Heat filled his face and bones as sweat and blood flowed from his torso. He lay motionless on the floor. He could hear what was being said but it sounded like he was in a tunnel and the words echoed in his brain.

"What the hell you do that for?" The lead officer screamed.

The rookie looked at his weapon and then to the limp body of Dandy Dee, "It went off accidently Murphy." He cried in a trembling voice.

"Call for an ambulance, and don't make any statements until we talk to the chief! It doesn't look good. He might not make it." Murphy barked.

Chapter 9

The Struggle is Real

For five days Dandy was in a comma fighting for his life. Schoolboy, Tyrone, and Freda were by his bedside daily hoping and praying. On the sixth day Dandy emerged victorious. He was conscious and recovering rapidly. His sight and speech returned but the doctors all agreed that he would never walk again. The bullet that tumbled by his spine left fragments lodged in his back and would leave him a paraplegic for life.

After a couple of days Schoolboy informed Tyrone that he would bear the bad news. His brother just couldn't muster the courage to tell him.

The following morning Schoolboy entered Dandy's room with a half smile and spoke cheerfully, "Hey youngster, how you feeling this morning?

Dandy retuned the smile as he looked up and said, "I feel fine, when do I raise up out this death bed?"

School dragged a chair close to Dandy's bedside and spoke calmly, "You just lay in the cut and rest up, your bail is posted so when you're able we'll talk about leaving."

"Dam, now I remember getting busted, but for what? Matter of fact what actually happened?"

School explained that he was arrested for possession of a controlled substance for sale. And that he was shot in the back while handcuffed. Dandy frowned and asked if they had a search warrant. School said he didn't know but had attorneys Johnson and Granville on top of it. He then asked, "Did you try to run?"

"Hell naw!" Dandy swore. "I didn't make any movements. They said they were Fed's and the next thing you know is I'm looking up at you and my brother's faces."

School gathered his words slowly, "Son, you know I don't bite my tongue about things and I always give you the real. The good or the bad."

Dandy was feeling lost and asked, "What's going on that I'm not hip to School? I know you and can tell you have something to tell me."

The old man continued, "Alright, if I didn't think you could handle it I wouldn't tell you. The bullet hit your spine and right now your legs aren't strong enough for you to walk. As you get stronger so will your legs." School didn't dare repeat the doctor's prognosis. Not yet anyway.

"So that's why I can't feel my feet. Give it to me straight School, will I ever walk again."

School held back the tears; he couldn't leave Dandy without the will to walk. And for the first time he told Dandy that he had a fifty-fifty chance. Not exactly a lie, but not the whole truth either. School wasn't a practicing religious man, but he was a believing man and knew God had the final call in all matters.

Dandy took it on the chin like a champ and said to School, "I hope to overcome this and get my wheels back again School, but I'm more concerned about this case and hoping I don't get railroaded. I know how the system can devour a man and warehouse him for life in some cases. This is the first time I really didn't do anything to deserve the time. But they say karma is a bitch. I've gotten away from a lot of things that I deserved to get punished for. If I have to do some time I will. I allowed myself to be in the position to get crossed. You taught me about position and Lefty did too, so I have no qualms. We will see what happens. But I can't put too much on my plate. I got to beat these charges and then worry about walking."

School felt a lot better about things and told Dandy, "You're absolutely right son. I just got this gut feeling that everything will turnout favorable for us. And you know how right I can be about hunches. Right now I'm going to roll outta here young soldier. Stay strong and keep your dukes up. I'll be back tomorrow with the attorneys. You just eat and rest. You've been in a lot of foul situations and came up smelling like a rose with very few exceptions."

With that said they embraced and looked forward to another day. School departed with a smile but he was frowning on the inside. He walked down the corridor to the elevators and stepped into the first one that stopped. He didn't know if it was going up or down, his mind was on Dandy and all the adversity he was up against. When he realized the elevator was going up and collecting passengers on every floor, it was too late, he had to go along for the ride.

A dignified young nurse entered the elevator while riffling through an armload of medical files.

"Sir would you please press number nine? She asked School.

"Sure thing Miss Jones." He replied after reading her nametag.

A doctor well into his forties spoke to the nurse when he came aboard on the sixth floor, "Hi Crystal, haven't seen you in awhile, how about lunch tomorrow?"

"Been really busy lately and have been grabbing lunch whenever I could, but sure, tomorrow sounds doable Dr. Lewis."

Schoolboy's mind clicked like a computer. Crystal Jones?...Crystal Jones...Crystal! He remembered where he had heard the name. No. It couldn't be, he thought to his self.

Just then the elevator flashed number nine and the door slide open. School held his hand on the door to keep it open and addressed the stranger, "Pardon me Miss Jones, I'm not trying to be flirtatious, as bad as I might have once wanted to, but do you know a fellow by the name of Dandy Dixon?"

She nearly dropped the files she held at the mention of Dandy's name. "No, I don't think so." She lied. Only because she knew Dandy was a product of the fast life and she didn't want to get involved or associated with anything he may have done.

"Pardon my intrusion young lady, I only asked because he is like a son and he would always speak about a Crystal Jones."

After feeling assured he wasn't the police, or some gangster looking for Dandy she opened up. "Pardon me sir, I do know a Dandy Dixon I just didn't know why you were asking if I knew him. Is he here at the hospital?"

"Yes he is, can we go to the cafeteria and talk?" School inquired.

Moments later they sat over coffee and tea for Crystal. "Dandy was shot by police and the doctors have stated that he may never walk again, matter of fact they said that he would not ever walk again." School explained.

Crystal was obviously moved by the news and tried to conceal her emotions. She listened as School explained the whole story, including that he told Dandy he had a chance to walk again with some therapy and courage because he didn't want him to feel totally defeated by what the doctors had said.

Crystal confessed, "God works in some of the strangest ways. Who would guess Dandy would wind up where I work and I'm the head therapist for patients in recovery. Lord! This seems so unreal, but on the other hand I believe in the power of God and know all things happens for a reason. I will have to pull some strings but don't worry Mr. Schoolboy, I'll do all I can."

***

The word was out and it traveled lightening fast. Early the next morning Dandy's room was adorned with flowers and balloons from the regulars at the Players Club. Lefty sent a telegram with words of encouragement along with a humungous fruit basket. Schoolboy packed a travel backpack with books and other reading materials along with a portable radio for his listening pleasure. Even ole Sweetmeat asked School if Dandy could have visitors.

The Panthers spearheaded protests followed by several civil rights groups and the media pertaining to Dandy being shot in the back while handcuffed. Word that the authorities were considering dropping all charges put a damper on things and eventually the spotlight moved on. But it was just a rumor.

Dandy was resting but his mind was racing, when Crystal walked into his room. He never looked past the white nurses uniform. She gazed at him as he peered out the window. "Sorry to interfere with your thoughts but can I bring you anything Mr. Dixon?" she softly asked.

Dandy whipped his body around and would have jumped to his feet if he were able. He sat up in the bed and shouted, "Crystal!" He just starred at her for a few seconds, befuddled about her presence and then asked, "I could use some fresh water. What are you doing here?" Before she could answer he added, "that's silly, I can see you're a nurse."

She smiled with a glow that lit up the room and stated, "Correct, I work here. When I received word of your accident I had to come see you. After all, patient and doctor should have a relaxed and confident level of communication amongst each other."

"You're a doctor?" Dandy asked.

"Something like that. I'm the head registered nurse over the Therapy Department and I have assigned myself to your rehab. You will be transferred to the ward this evening and we will start therapy tomorrow." She stated.

"Well Beautiful, once again the fickle hand of fate has been dropped on us." Dandy said.

Blushing and trying to remain as professional as possible Crystal answered, "Yes, it seems to be in the cards." After about twenty minutes of conversation she announced, "I have to go now but I will see you tomorrow."

Tomorrow couldn't come fast enough for both of them. Although Dandy's prognosis wasn't encouraging, Crystal refused to accept defeat. And she didn't want to instill any in Dandy's mind. She had witnessed many miracles and knew the mind was a powerful weapon against adversity. Especially when combined with prayer.

The next morning before School and the lawyers had a chance to see him, Dandy had other visitors, two men with government written all over them. One was White and the other was Black. Both were neatly dressed in business suits and ties.

With a bourgeois twang in his vocabulary the Black agent came off as a cop just working to keep meat on the dinner table for his family. "Good morning Mr. Dixon, I'm agent Joe Burns," as he passed his card to Dandy and continued, "This is my partner agent Kelly," pointing to his colleague.

Agent Kelly took the baton and flexed in a more authoritative voice, "We are from internal affairs," while flashing government badges.

Dandy was keenly observant and remained silent.

Kelly continued, "Agent Redford has stated that his gun discharged accidently during the process of detaining you on August fifteenth. We have been authorized to have all criminal charges against you dismissed provided you sign this affidavit nullifying any future law suit you may file in regards to the accident."

Dandy voiced his position. "If I wasn't handcuffed when it took place you would say I was running or resisting arrest. I'm not signing nothing until I speak with my counsel. I haven't been convicted of any crime. Not yet anyway, and probably won't be."

Agent Burns took the floor, "You absolutely have a right not to say anything or sign the agreement."

An angry Dandy said, "If, and I say if I am convicted I'll do the time but you will pay dearly thru the nose! My physical handicap and not to mention my mental anguish is worth more than the million dollar words one of your sharp lawyer uses."

Agent Kelly regained the floor, "Mr. Dixon, we don't come for an arrest until we are ready. And we have a nearly one hundred percent rate of conviction. You sir have been under investigation for some time. You will do the time if convicted and then you may even win a law suit, is that correct?"

Dandy replied, "I'm listening, I'm not talking."

The agent starred coldly and cracked a devious smile and dropped the bomb on him. "We haven't mentioned the pending charges of income tax evasion. But sleep on it, we'll be back in the morning."

Dandy was stymied. After all the advise and instructions that Lefty and School had laid on him, and not to mention one of the mafia bosses telling him to set up a business and start paying taxes as he made money. But he had allowed himself to get caught with his drawers down. He had procrastinated too long thinking he had plenty of time to put his business in order. Was this a fatal mistake? Had he crossed his own self?

***

That next morning, during their therapy session Dandy demanded, "Listen Crystal, I want you to lay the truth on me. Am I ever going to walk again? This process is moving too slowly for me; I'm a get up and go type of guy. I know the twitching provides a slight feeling like I said, but I need to get cracking and rolling again."

"You must trust and believe in the process Dandy. Rest your mind as well as your body after a long day of therapy. Sometimes God will take you thru the fire in order to come out healed. If you cut yourself it takes time for the wound to form a scab and heal, and that scab will make the skin tougher. Just keep fighting and think positive. When you go to sleep pray for positive dreams of running up and down the basketball court, going hiking or swimming. I'm here for you and will do everything in my power to assist your comeback."

"Oh and while your on that subject. I appreciate every ounce of concern you give me but what about your husband and your home life? Are you a mother as well?"

It was some of the questions that Crystal knew she had to address one day. And it looked like the day had arrived. She did spend most of her time and intended to spend more time taking care of Dandy. But she wasn't quite ready to talk about her home life. Reliving how her focus shifted after her mother's passing and the feelings of loneliness. But she also knew she needed to clear the table and set the record straight.

Just then, Schoolboy and Tyrone burst into the therapy room with smiles. "How's it going lil brother? You looking better." Tyrone said.

"You would too with a pretty young tender and educated sister taking care of you." School confirmed.

"We came to tell you that the lawyers think they can salvage some of your holdings, not much but a little something is better than a whole lot of nothing." Tyrone declared.

The agents overheard the conversation as they also stepped into the room.

Agent Kelly pressed on, "As we informed you yesterday Mr. Dixon, you will loose all of your assets, and basically everything you own. And you will still wind up owing Uncle Sam restitution. Also, you will have to do the time it carries."

Dandy was speechless as the agent unfolded more information, "So sir, this exchange is a bargain. You loose everything, but you will have your freedom."

School and Tyrone looked on in bewilderment.

Agent Burns pulled a pen from his coat pocket and resumed, "Personally we don't care which route you take. We're assigned to present the offer and that's all. You appear to be a rational thinking man and if it were me I would accept the offer. We don't want the bad publicity and hours of court litigation, and red tape to boot. You on the other hand will retain something more valuable than gold. Freedom."

Suddenly Dandy's two lawyers entered the crowded room. After repeating the conditions of the deal, the attorneys verified everything in writing and had the documents signed. They knew it was in Dandy's best interest to accept the deal. The drug case could have possibly been beat. It was the evidence contained in the indictment of income tax evasion that was irrefutable.

Everything was to be confiscated. And Dandy had to accept a year of unsupervised parole, which wasn't bad, and the fine was suspended. By the government knowing Dandy would be a paraplegic for life they didn't want to have to shell out millions of dollars down the line. The freedom from any jail time most definitely wasn't out of any form of compassion whatsoever. It all revolved around money.

School followed up with "The shade of a toothpick beats the hot blazing sun."

"Your sis sent you a plate of food lil brother and we gonna get out the way and let the beautiful lady do her job. We just wanted to bring the food and put you up on events." Tyrone announced.

School added, "Okay son we out of here, hang on in there and keep your best foot forward in every situation. Even Mary was instructed to shake the tree to make the fruit fall."

After everyone left Dandy looked at Crystal and said, "So I had asked you some questions before my visitors arrived."

She spoke slowly, "I am no longer married Dandy. It didn't work out. We were together for less than a year and no I don't have any children. Before you ask I'll say that my ex was a pathological liar and I can't deal with any person that is not honest. One thing is for sure and another for certain, I gave it my all and tried to make it work. I do want children and a few of them. I was an only child and I always wanted siblings. So there it is Mr. Dixon, now you know why and how I have so much free time – time that I choose to give towards helping you."

Dandy was more comfortable with their patient/doctor status and asked, "Where do we go from here when I have recovered and won't need the excellent service you give me."

"That's the million dollar question. You're the master of the game "cousin", you tell me. But not now, we have to finish your session. I had to tell administration that you were my cousin so that they wouldn't object to the time I spend with you."

***

Crystal was more engaged than ever. She spent less time at her house and more with Dandy. After a whirlpool bath one afternoon Dandy wanted to try and stand along the parallel rail without any assistance. He was very shaky but he did manage to stand holding on to the railing. Crystal was ecstatic and it really kicked her hope up high.

After a few more weeks Dandy stood holding onto the support as Crystal patiently yet persistently urged him to hold on and take a step. Dandy put a foot forward and tried to advance. The little strength he had in his knees wasn't accustomed to the foreign pressure of the off balance step and he collapsed to the floor.

He cursed and said, "I can't do this, its no use."

His words were like a knife in the back and tears rolled down her cheeks as she yelled, "Get up and walk Dandy! You can do it. Don't ever say you can't. Get up now!"

Dandy looked up and said, "Say! Who do you think you shouting at?"

Crystal didn't lighten up, "YOU! The great Dandy Dee, remember him? The man who will walk." Dee was amazed at her drive and instantly came to the realization that she was right. His pride was afflicted by this dedicated woman who had now kneeled down on the floor next to him and said, "We both getting up together."

They were on the floor face to face when Dandy mugged her and pressed his lips on hers and darted his tongue in and around her mouth. She flung both arms around him and returned the kiss like they were doing the tango. He slowed the rhythm and she followed. He gently sucked her bottom lip and then the top lip. He then ran his moist weapon of love around her ear and down her neck with the tip.

Crystal was on fire inside and just as she reached her highest peak he pulled back while looking her square into her glossy eyes and said, "We got to get up, remember."

Slightly embarrassed she agreed, "Yes, this isn't the most appropriate position to be caught in." She helped him struggle back to his feet. It was an exhausting challenge for them both.

He could barely speak but he finally spoke in a soft and calm tone, "And another thing. Don't ever raise your voice higher than mine. If I shout at you, you can shout back but not with a higher volume than mine, understood?"

He smiled after saying that and she smiled back and said, "Yes sir Captain…I mean cousin. And please don't make contact with me like that again at this workplace, it's not professional."

"You are right and I'm not too big a man whereas I can't admit when I'm wrong. It was a spontaneous act and I would love to do it again but at the right time and place." He confessed.

"And I wouldn't object one bit, sir."

"It appears that we don't have to do any more talking. I am quite aware of your feelings for me. That never really was the question. I had a partner back in the life named Phillip and we called him Overkill Phil. He was, and still is a boss player with a fair stable but he could have twice as many ladies. But he didn't because he would talk his way in and keep talking till he talked his way right on out. My point is, the signs are on the wall and a blind man could see how much I adore you." Dandy said smoothly.

"Keep on talking, you make it sound so good. I see why those ladies flocked to you." She confessed.

110

"Actually I turned down quite a few for various reasons. My mannerism did the talking and my style is more conservative than most players." He explained.

"Well you go ahead on Mack Daddy." She teased.

"No Crystal, I'm saying we can hash out some kind of commitment to one another later. And we can see what level we want it to be on but now I need to stand tall and walk before I can put anything else on my mind. You say I will walk and I have full trust in you but I need to have full trust and confidence by actually being able to walk. And that's just me. I know dudes with more game and heart with no legs, than ten with legs. My homeboy Puppet, The Magnificent Puppet we called him, was a pimp rolling in a wheel chair. He danced in that chair, he drove a big Cadillac with hand controls, and I have seen his women fight over who would push him in his chair. The lack of being able to walk wasn't a handicap at all for him. But I don't know if I want to be responsible for your safety if I can't walk. Maybe I would, or probably not because I am not in that position as of yet and don't know for sure. So let's handle our future like we dealing with my therapy. A step at a time."

Chapter 10

The Golden Proposition

The months rolled by and after nearly a year of treatment with tender loving care attached Dandy walked out of the hospital with the assistance of a walker but nevertheless, upright and on his own.

He and Crystal agreed that he would stay with her at her house off Third and Western in the Wilshire district. His car, home, businesses, and bank accounts were all seized. He did have a decent stash of cash that Schoolboy had held for him. And a few small items of jewelry and clothes he left at his brother's place. He forgot about paying taxes but remembered the po' rat with only one hole to stash stuff in.

Back to the starting blocks of life he moved past the mistakes and bad breaks. He understood one thing very well; the hand he was dealt was the one his hands created. Other than Priscilla, he had no one to blame but himself. And even Priscilla's actions manifested from his lack of ability to see her turning sour.

Crystal wanted him to basically square up and raise a family. He couldn't blame her. She was a good woman and deserved as much. But, he didn't know if he was ready for it. He had tasted too much of the good life, a life that was really a dream. Lefty used to say that this life was nothing but a dream that fades away. He just hadn't reached that level of consciousness yet. He lived too much of the life of leisure to settle for a subpar lifestyle.

But just what he would do was still unknown. Schoolboy suggested that he fully recover before talking about a game plan. After weeks of tossing and turning at night he came up with a plan.

***

From the walker to a cane and then finally steps on his own. It was over a year but now Dandy was walking independently, a victory both physically and mentally. The first thing he did was to take a trip back to his old neighborhood.

His brother was at work but Freda and the kids screamed in delight at Dandy's arrival. After a piece of Freda's award winning German Chocolate Cake and a cup of decaffeinated coffee Dandy stood up, "Dang Sis. You get better with time; the cake was a hit with my taste buds. I'm going to leave the car parked here and take a stroll to Schoolboy's. I need to walk and digest that delightful indulgence I didn't need."

Freda chuckled and said, "I heard what you said. Take your time, we are not going anywhere."

The block hadn't changed one bit. After waving at neighbors and stopping to exchange greetings with others Dandy finally reached the end of the block and spun around onto San Pedro Street. Just off the corner he walked into School's joint. "What up with it?" He announced with a broad smile and open arms.

"My son! This is a pleasant surprise. How you and Crystal getting along?" School wanted to know. "You just don't know how happy I am to see you back on your feet again. When you first went into the hospital the doctors told us you probably wouldn't ever walk again."

In shock, Dandy was lost for words and short of breath. After a few seconds he spoke, "I never knew that. No one ever told me, not even you School.

"No I didn't, you didn't need any negativity in your mind." He explained.

"And Crystal put all that work in on me not knowing if I would make it or not? You just cast a different light on things. I can't thank you enough."

"It's Crystal that deserves the applauds son. And you know I'm not quick to decorate no dame, but you have a keeper there. I know you have been let down and disappointed in the past but I believe there's a future with her."

Dandy was silent and nodded in approval. He exchanged farewells and proceeded on up San Pedro. Passing the liquor store Sweetmeat rushed up behind him and screamed, "Dandy! I thought you was Nulson for a minute. You don't know how happy I am to see you walking in these streets again."

"Thanks Sweetmeat, me and you both are happy. And thanks for asking about my health. I appreciate it."

"I need two dollars Dandy, can you help me out. I ran a little short today." Sweetmeat asked.

Dandy dug into his slide and peeled a saw buck off a small roll, " After you get your drink go to Momma Jacobs Café up the street and get the special. A piece of chicken, some read beans n' rice, and a piece of cornbread with some greens for three dollars. You need something to stick to your stomach."

"That's why I love you Dandy, Thanks."

Dandy continued up San Pedro past the poolroom and stopped in front of the Golden Ring Gambling Hall. He had to socialize for a few minutes with Six Toe Red, Stack A Dollar, and Keno, who were on the sidewalk planning a trip to the Kotch Ball in Mobile Alabama. They were elated to see him walking. "Hey Double Dee! Man its good to see you up and moving around again." Stack A Dollar declared.

"Real talk Dee," Six Toe Red affirmed.

"No bull shit. We constantly send those 'player prayers' up for you" Keno vowed.

After hugs and high fives Dandy lit on up "Pedro" past the Top Hat Motel and the Frosty Freeze. He then swung into the doors of Fremont High. On through the halls of the administration building, which brought back so many memories, he opened another smaller door, which said, "Night School Enrollment."

***

Dandy was alarmed when the message from Schoolboy was labeled urgent. That was akin to a tactical alert, or a red flag alert from the military. Dandy couldn't get across town quick enough for his satisfaction.

Was School up against impending danger? Did he hit the jackpot and need an armored car or had some other huge stroke of good fortune? Different scenarios danced in his head.

He parked Crystal's ride and bust into School's joint. "What's going on School? You okay?" He shouted.

115

"I'm doing very well thank you, and so are you." School declared.

"You had me nervous School, and what you mean 'I'm okay too'?"

"Patty, the bartender at the Player's Club, sent word that a very wealthy looking white business woman was inquiring about your whereabouts."

"So how did the bartender know she was well off?" Dandy asked.

"You know how women can size another dame up as soon as she enters a room? She said ole girl had a seven thousand dollar suit on, fifteen hundred dollar shoes and diamonds on every finger. She even knew the brand names but I forgot what she said. But this here is a business card she left for you to contact her." School said as he handed Dandy the information.

Dandy looked at the card and immediately recognized the name. It was Laura, the German lady he had back in '71. When he called the number a secretary conveyed Ms. Laura Kaufman's request that Dandy meet her the next night for dinner at the Brown Derby restaurant in Hollywood at Vine and Hollywood Boulevard at eight P.M.

The following evening Dandy was freshly attired in a pin stripped Giorgio Armani suit as he sat in the lobby waiting for his dinner date. After checking the time he walked to the front entrance just as a Pearl White 1976 Silver Shadow Rolls hit the curb for the valet who rushed to open the rear door.

Laura stepped on the sidewalk with a smile as she locked her focus on Dandy. Without looking at the valet she stated, "My driver will attend to the car."

Dandy walked calmly toward her and took her hand to help her support her stance. She was stunning in a Saint John gold leaf brocade knit suit. Dandy stood six-foot one and she was six-feet but the Christian Louboutin red spiked heels had her towering over Dandy by an inch or two. Her diamond brocade necklace had to be seven or eight carats. And had huge diamonds on every finger that glistened under the neon lights nearly blinding Dandy. His days of old began to surface and for the first time in a long while he was thirsty for the game.

At the dining table Laura ordered a surf and turf steak, medium rare and a glass of Chateau Latour wine. Dandy had blackened salmon with shrimp, crawfish and crabmeat layered on top with mountain spring water and lemon.

While waiting Dandy broke the silence, "It appears you have done very well for yourself over the last few years. Or has it been longer since we laid eyes on one another?"

"Let me explain so that you clearly understand everything that has transpired. When Priscilla and her sidekick Duchess flipped on you the Feds wanted me, Stormy, Carmen and Red to jump aboard the betrayal ship. We refused them and as a result the girls were booked on some bogus solicitation charges that were dropped the next day. Unfortunately I had an old warrant for a boosting case I caught way back before I chose you."

"What happened after that," Dandy inquired.

"I'm getting there Daddy," she declared and resumed, "Let me back up a bit I never ran my full pedigree down to you because we were such a perfect combination and our ship was sailing so smoothly that I didn't see or feel we had a need to talk any more than what we did. I came to this country from Germany, which you know, but I didn't tell you I was here on a student visa. I was enrolled at the University of Illinois. My parents paid my tuition, expenses, and provided a small allowance. After I received my Bachelor's Degree in Business I was ready to open a business of my own in the fashion arena. My parents blew it and demanded that I stay in school and obtain a Master's Degree. I was tired of the books and wanted to spread my wings. We had a huge argument and my rebellion began. I was living on my own because they cut off all assistance. I had a small savings but the fast life was intriguing to me. Anything to buck the system turned me on. So that's when I met you Mr. Dandy Dee."

"Very interesting Laura, it sounds like you could write a book about your life, but go ahead and continue." Dandy said.

"So as I was saying, after the little six months county time with sixty days off for good behavior I was deported back to Germany. My parents were furious but didn't know why I was returned home. I finally agreed to finish my education and they immediately began the process for my re-entry into the States and re-enrollment in college. My parents put thousands of dollars into the U.S. economy. So back I came and started working on my Master's Degree while operating a retail clothing manufacturing business that I own, which was set up by my dad."

"Sounds good to me. You have certainly been blessed." Dandy confirmed.

Dinner was served and the conversation continued, "My income was substantial but tragedy struck hard and heavy, all of a sudden."

Her eyes began to tear and Dandy raised one curious eyebrow while awaiting the next words out her mouth.

"My mother and father were both killed in a horrific car accident in Munich." With a deep sigh she added, "I inherited millions of dollars from the stock in BMW that my father owned, and the life insurance policies that my parents had were very lucrative as well. I am set for life Dandy. I've been traveling the world on one big vacation after the other, buying all that pleases my eyes." She confessed.

"My deepest condolences to you. No amount of money can fill the void in your heart, or take the place of your parents. On the sunny side I can truly say I know a millionaires." Dandy voiced with slight glee.

"You can say that you and your woman are millionaires if you so desire." She announced and awaited reply.

"And if I accept you?" He asked.

"You will never want for anything Dandy. I'm tired of the trips and spending sprees by myself. I need companionship and do not desire to run thru a bunch of men to find the right one," She answered.

"I'm grateful that you thought enough of ole Dandy to seek and find me." He stated.

"It wasn't hard once I hired the right people." She affirmed.

Dandy's mind was racing like it was on the track of the Indy 500. She needed a swift decision but he didn't have one. Five or six years ago he would leap over a wild herd of horses to cop a score like Laura without an ounce of hesitation whatsoever. He would be held in high esteem amongst his peers. But he hesitated. He didn't know why, but he did. He wouldn't ever have to break the law again in life. He needed consultation with the old master.

"Let me sleep on it Laura. It's not the sex, it's the time you want from me." He explained.

The drink was creeping and she added with a coy smile, "Hmmmm, both would be delightful. But I realize this is a sudden, drop everything else you're doing type of situation. When can you decide Mr. Delightful?"

Dandy was smooth and had never allowed a woman, or a man for that matter, see him sweat. He immediately re-grouped and took control. "I have your number and I'll give you mine. I'll let you know in due time. About a few days."

"Okay, I understand, meanwhile here is a little present I picked up for you." She voiced while reaching for an oblong gift box.

Dandy took the box and opened it up. It was a solid gold diamond studded Patek Philippe wristwatch. "Thank you my dear, you have exquisite taste." He graciously admitted, knowing it cost about fifty-thousand.

"If I hear back from you it's just the beginning of welcome home presents. If I do not hear from you consider it a goodbye present." She sadly admitted.

"No! It might be a welcome home present. Or a so long, see you some other spring type of present cause all goodbyes ain't never gone." He said and continued, "Thank you again for the gift. It's very rude not to accept an offering, and I still don't turn nothing down but my collar."

They stood and embraced before departing. Dandy didn't know if he would ever see her again, see her everyday for the rest of his life, or play her for a short duration of time.

After running the entire spill down to Schoolboy, the old master exploded, "Men pray for the position you're in, not just players but squares too have enough vision to spot a goldmine. Are you loosing it? You are a Black man in America with a filthy rich White woman willing to make you an instant millionaire and give you the world. No, forget her being a White woman; she's a green woman! Hell she could be purple with polka dots all over her body. Why you fudging and hesitating? Have you forgot how to play? Never close an open door!"

"No School, I ain't forgot any lesson or how to play. It's just…" He hesitated. "I have all I need. For some reason all I want doesn't carry as much weight as it once did. This last bust didn't carry a life sentence so I could have reluctantly done the bit and jumped right back in the game. But being cripple for the rest of my life was a situation I would have had doubts about living with so I made a pledge to a Higher Source, actually an agreement to be a more morally conscious man if I recovered. It really humbled me School. I had no idea I wasn't supposed to walk again, I though it was temporary. Crystal was treating me night and day. I feel like God put wings on her and assigned her to me."

School smiled and confessed, "That's what I really wanted to hear. I had to put the full court press on you."

"No, you had my head in a full nelson." Dandy countered.

"Well I wanted to hear you say how you really felt. Now you can get out the way and allow another player to step in your boots. But damn! The dame has a serious itch for you. You're leaving a lot on the table but then again, all money ain't good…sometimes."

Dandy nodded in approval as they exchanged farewells. He returned to his brother's house after deep reflection with every step. When he got back home to Crystal he shared the conversation he had with Laura.

Crystal asked, "Well what are you going to do Dandy?"

"I'll tell you after I graduate from night school."

"I'm glad you're graduating soon because I'm not waiting another ten plus years "cousin"." Crystal stated arrogantly.

To which Dandy had no reply.

***

Days rolled into weeks and after a few months Dandy received a wedding invitation with full flight and hotel accommodations from Laura. The wedding was taking place in a couple of months at the Hotel Le Fouquett in the heart of Paris; a swanky upscale joint that only the elite could afford.

Laura attached a note stating that she still felt compelled to let him be aware of her decisions. And explained that she met and hooked a very wealthy oil tycoon from the Middle East. He was young and compatible so she felt like she should tie the knot while time was on her side.

Being the gentleman that he was, Dandy sent a congratulations card.

"Thank you for the request but I won't be able to attend such a memorable event. I'm sending high hopes of a very abundantly happy and secure future in spirit. Love from Double Dee P.S. Maybe some other spring will blossom for us."

Dandy doubted he would ever see her again but remembered to leave a crack in the doorway.

***

The auditorium at Fremont High was nearly full on the evening of Night School Graduation. Tyrone, Freda, the boys, and Fatima were in attendance. His cousin Leonard was also in town and made his presence known. Schoolboy proudly sat waiting for the ceremonies to begin. Crystal was more excited than Dandy. "Po Boy," "Love," "Cleve," and "Ace" along with a few more of Dandy's homeboys he had grown up with were there to cheer him on. Even ole Sweetmeat was smiling.

MaDear's wish, or command, was coming to fruition. Dandy's name was announced. He stood tall and stepped lively toward the podium with a prize-winning smile. It was more than a high school diploma. It was his mother's smiling face looking down on him that created a warm feeling of joy in his heart. It wasn't a Master's Degree but it held much more acclaim and honor to Dandy.

The principal handed Dandy the diploma that reminded him of a baton that would mentally accelerate him forward the rest of his life. Just knowing his MaDear would be overly joyful was a soothing thought. The auditorium exploded with cheers.

When the noise subsided Dandy took the microphone and told Crystal to approach the floor. She was amazed and caught off guard. Very slowly but surely she stepped to the stage. Dandy assisted her as he took her hand while she climbed the steps. He then pulled a wedding ring out its case. Crystal was wide-eyed and speechless. The tears flowed and she hugged Dandy and wouldn't let go. In moments a pre-paid reverend joined them to perform wedding vows.

Dandy never asked her to marry him in the traditional manner. But she had no objections and said "I do" before the man with the white, round collar finished asking if she took Dandy for her husband.

Dandy also vowed with an "I do" and whispered to Crystal, "Despite turbulent times, if something is written to be, it's going to be. You wrote me a long time ago in a letter and said, 'All good byes ain't gone'."

THE END...

Made in the USA
Middletown, DE
29 April 2021